Second Chance in Summit County

Second Chance in Summit County

Summit County Series, Book 1

By Katherine Karrol

Second Chance in Summit County

Copyright © 2018 Katherine Karrol

Contents

Second Chance in Summit County

Title Page

Copyright

Chapter 1   1

Chapter 2   4

Chapter 3   7

Chapter 4   9

Chapter 5   11

Chapter 6   16

Chapter 7   19

Chapter 8   22

Chapter 9   25

Chapter 10   27

Chapter 11   30

Chapter 12   32

Chapter 13   34

Chapter 14   36

Chapter 15   39

Chapter 16   42

Chapter 17   43

Chapter 18	45
Chapter 19	47
Chapter 20	49
Chapter 21	51
Chapter 22	53
Chapter 23	56
Chapter 24	62
Chapter 25	65
Chapter 26	68
Chapter 27	70
Chapter 28	72
Chapter 29	74
Chapter 30	76
Chapter 31	79
Chapter 32	82
Chapter 33	84
Chapter 34	87
Chapter 35	88
Chapter 36	91
Chapter 37	93
Chapter 38	96
Chapter 39	98
Chapter 40	101
Chapter 41	105
Chapter 42	107
Chapter 43	109
Chapter 44	111
Chapter 45	113

Chapter 46   116

Dear Reader,   119

Summit County Series, Book 2   121

About the Author   123

About the Summit County Series   125

Books in the Summit County Series   127

Chapter 1

What was she thinking? Emily had been driving for hours and hadn't heard one thing about where to go.

Why did I think He would take me to the perfect hiding place? Do I really think He's going to give me Old-Testament-hearing-His-voice-style guidance after what I've done? Maybe this was a crazy idea.

"Lord, I'm sorry for treating You like my personal vending machine. I'm sorry for asking You to give me answers and guidance I don't deserve. I guess it was my voice I was hearing, not Yours. Well, at least it was a pretty drive."

Pretty didn't even begin to describe what the drive had been. The farther north and west she drove on the two-lane highways, the more hints and spots of color she saw on the trees. It was just after Labor Day and fall was starting to show itself. Every time she drove over a hill, she let out an involuntary "Wow!"

It had been a couple of years since she had been able to visit her parents in the fall, and she drank in the scenery. Of all the things she missed about Michigan, fall color and coolness and everything that went with it topped the list.

The small towns and middle-of-nowhere motels she had seen while driving all day were charming and drew her like a magnet, but none of them were *the* place. She thought for sure she'd heard God say to go home to Michigan and He would show her the town

He would give her a new life in. She thought for sure He would lead her back to a town up north like the one she'd spent a week in as a teenager with a friend. It was a good thing that she wasn't looking for that specific town, because she had no idea where it was or even what it was called.

"When I left Mom and Dad's house this morning, I was sure You were going to take me on an adventure and take me to my new home. They thought I was a little out there, but I was certain I was following Your lead."

She'd thought for sure God had accepted her into His personal witness protection program, someplace where no one had heard of Colin Meissner, let alone his wife who just *must have known* everything that he was doing – his wife who, according to local gossips and social media, was equally culpable for his crimes and moral failures, even though they were committed in secret.

"Is it too much to ask to send me to a town that doesn't have the internet?" *Yes, it's too much. Stop asking for things and be thankful He got you out of LA. He doesn't owe you anything, let alone a perfectly clean slate. He's giving you a fresh start. Show some gratitude.*

"Thank You, Lord. Thank You for getting me out of LA. Thank you for the nice visit with Mom and Dad. Thank You for giving me the hint that I needed to be stashing money away and giving me enough time to gather enough to make this trip. Thank You for giving me a chance to have a new start. I know it won't be perfect, and it most certainly won't be easy, but it will be new."

The longer she drove, the more she talked. "This time I won't be shutting You out. I paid a hefty price for doing that. I ignored Your warnings, along with everyone else's, about marrying Colin, and I won't do that again. Let's just find a town that has a cheap motel I can sleep in tonight. Maybe I can get a decent night's sleep and You'll tell me tomorrow where to go next. If I hear nothing, I can go back to Mom and Dad's for another couple of days and regroup."

She passed a sign that said "Welcome to Summit County." As long as it wasn't LA, it was fine with her.

She wanted to leave everything from there behind. That's why she had only taken her clothes and the possessions she had before she met Colin when she left. It was her way of shaking the dust off her feet when she left that town and life behind.

She looked forward to the day when she would be able to shake everything off. That is, *if* she could shake everything off. *How do you shake off scandal and shame and public humiliation? How do you shake off being completely blind to the person you married and lived with for five years? How do you shake the feeling that if you'd paid attention to things better, you could have prevented others from being hurt?*

Their pain was hanging like a cloud over her. That was the worst part. It was the others whose lives *her* husband had ruined. She had ruined her own by her poor choices; *he* had ruined others' by his abusive – and criminal – activity. And she had been so blind to it that she'd done nothing to stop it.

She wiped a tear from her eye. Here she was, trying to start over, and she was already feeling defeated. How was she supposed to start over when the past followed her in her head?

Chapter 2

When she saw a sign that said "Hideaway – 5 Miles," she chuckled. "That seems like exactly the kind of town I'm looking for. I know, Lord. That would be a little obvious. Thanks for the laugh, though. Now can You please provide a clean motel in this town?"

The rolling hills as she got closer just made the last stretch of the drive better.

She approached a large hill with a huge white gateway looming over it with lighthouses on either side of the two lane road. "I guess I've reached Hideaway. I have to admit, that gateway is pretty cool."

As the little Honda crested the hill and she caught her first glimpse of the tiny town, her breath caught and the heaviness she had been feeling lifted. It was like a hidden pocket of heaven surrounded by large forested hills.

Hideaway.

From the small bay scattered with sailboats and fishing boats on the left to the white steeple peeking above the houses and trees straight ahead, it was as if the town was stuck in a time capsule from days gone by and it beckoned her to keep driving. Lake Michigan lay at the far end of the town like a protective barrier from the outside world and the lighthouse that inspired the gateway stood tall at the end of a long pier. She felt a peace sweep over her for the first time in recent memory as she drove down the big hill toward the steeple.

The two-lane highway that took her into the town turned into a neighborhood street without fanfare, as if that's what highways do. The businesses and homes lining the street were all well-kept and had their own unique charm. There were a few antique stores, a grocery store, and a mom-and-pop diner welcoming visitors. The houses were mostly a mix of Victorian and Craftsman, and a few cottages were sprinkled in for good measure. All fit together perfectly, like a painting of what small towns should look like.

This might be the place.

She took note of the quaint, well-kept motel on the right, especially of its vacancy sign, and kept driving. She pulled over to the side of the road where she had a nice view of the small but commanding church. It had to be at least a hundred and fifty years old, and its colonial pillars and tall steeple were the stuff of postcards. There was something so comforting about the place. It was just a building, but it felt like salve to her soul to sit and stare at it.

She tried to remember the last time she'd been in a church; it had been a while. She had been active in her church in Newport Beach when she was young and single, but when she married Colin and they moved to Culver City to be closer to work, it got more and more difficult to get there. It was harder going alone and trying to dodge the questions from friends about where her new husband was. She tried a few churches near their new home, but felt even more isolated walking in alone. By that time, he had stopped making excuses for not going with her and it became easier to watch the live stream of her church at home. Eventually it became painful to do so. She started watching podcasts of sermons from other churches, but even that lost its spot in her routine as Colin started making more and more plans for them on Sundays.

∞∞∞

After sitting and staring at the church for quite some time, she suddenly noticed that the sun was lowering toward the horizon. She headed toward the downtown area, looking for food. If she timed it right, she could grab some takeout and get to the beach for sunset. The one thing she liked about LA was the sunset; it was the only thing she was going to miss.

Maybe if she stayed in Hideaway, she wouldn't need to miss anything.

Chapter 3

*T*his is absolutely amazing. This is going down in my autobiography as the most perfect sunset ever.

She munched on the taco she'd gotten at the food truck and watched the sun as it colored the clouds. The reds, corals, and pinks were stunning. She didn't want to ruin the simplicity of the moment by getting her phone out for a picture, so she studied the sunset in an attempt to memorize it. The slight chill in the air didn't even bother her. It was worth getting to sit on a bench and breathe the fresh air as she listened to the waves lap against the shore.

She watched the couples and families walking out on the pier, snapping pictures of the sky and of each other. Watching them struggle to get enough cell signals out by the stately lighthouse to Instagram their pictures made her giggle.

"I guess you're just going to have to enjoy this beauty without seeing how many likes you get for a while, folks."

When the sun went over the horizon, she realized she needed to find a place to sleep. She wished the little motel was closer to the beach so she could listen to the waves all night.

As she walked toward her car, a weathered bed and breakfast sign down the block from the beach caught her eye. *Shoreside Inn. What a perfect name for a place like that.*

It was a beautiful old Victorian home with a large and inviting front porch. She could tell it had been a while since it had been painted, but it still had the soft polychrome paint scheme she always loved to see on Victorians. Before she knew it, she was standing in front of it.

She was about to walk up the steps when she realized that a stay at a bed and breakfast, even a weathered one, would not stretch her limited dollars as much as the tiny motel would. She turned around and almost bumped into an elderly woman with kind eyes and a smile that made her feel as if she had known her for years.

"Oh! I'm sorry, ma'am. I was lost in thought and didn't hear you behind me."

"That's quite all right, dear. I'm a bit tired and wasn't paying much attention either. Are you looking for a room? I'm afraid we only have one left with it being this close to Labor Day, and it's quite tiny."

"Actually, if it's tiny enough, it might fit perfectly into my tiny budget."

Chapter 4

She woke up to the smell of bacon. It was even better than the smell of fresh-baked chocolate chip cookies that had greeted her in the foyer the night before.

"Thank you, Lord, for this day. Thank You for tiny rooms in run-down bed and breakfasts and sweet little old ladies who give good deals to tired wanderers who are willing to clean their own rooms. And thank You for bacon."

She rifled through her suitcase and found a green shirt that had the perfect combination of texture and pattern to hide the wrinkles. A pair of jeans, hair clip to subdue her long auburn waves, and slip on sandals made her presentable enough for breakfast.

There were two couples in the dining room when she walked in and all four greeted her with warm smiles. *I forgot how nice people act in small towns.*

"Good Mornings" were exchanged and she found a seat. Breakfast was served family style and she was happy to see that there was plenty of coffee left, along with the now-famous-in-her-head bacon, scrambled eggs, hash browns, pastries, and fruit.

She chatted with the others and carefully kept the conversation on them. She had learned a long time ago that she could avoid giving information about herself if she kept asking questions. It was what made people say she was a great conversationalist. She had also learned by accident that she found others' lives more interesting than her own – well, at least less depressing.

Not only had she successfully avoided giving any information about herself apart from her name and first-time visitor status, but she found out about the other guests and the once-glorious home she was staying in.

The Mortons had spent their honeymoon there thirty-two years ago and had come back for every anniversary. The Parkers had only been able to make it from Arizona about every four or five years, but had been coming even longer than the Mortons. It was clear that they loved the place and thought of Mrs. Glover as family. The Mortons had even come for Mr. Glover's memorial service last year. The sadness was apparent on their faces when they spoke in hushed tones about how long Mrs. Glover would be able to keep the place running.

She was doing an amazing job of keeping everything tidy and making her guests feel like family, but the home was old and was in need of some upkeep that she would not be able to do alone and probably didn't have the money to hire out. If not for a local handyman who made necessary repairs for her in exchange for home-cooked meals, the place would be falling into disrepair.

Chapter 5

After breakfast, Emily helped Mrs. Glover clean up the dining room and kitchen. It was hard to convince the sweet woman to let her, but she prevailed. At least she thought she did. She still had a sneaking suspicion that Mrs. Glover had backed down because she saw that Emily needed something to do. She had a way about her, a deep wisdom and discernment – she was part Mrs. Claus and part prophet. Seeing her in the daylight made her look less like Mrs. Claus, but she still had a warm, grandmotherly way about her even if she was younger than Emily initially thought.

Emily had made the decision to stay at least one more night so that she could spend some time talking to God and listening for His direction on whether to stay there or not. She also wanted to enjoy the town for just a little while longer. *Please let me stay, Lord. Please let me stay.*

They chatted about the house and the town while they cleaned up and Emily learned that the home had been in Mrs. Glover's family for generations. Her great-great grandfather got into the logging business at the right time and had built a house so that he could board his fellow workers.

When his own logging business took off and he didn't need boarders, he leveled it and rebuilt a grand home to raise his family in. It had stayed in the family through the generations and Mrs. Glover had spent summers there as a child, living the rest of the year downstate near Detroit. Her parents decided to retire in Hideaway and moved in with her grandfather to take care of him in his last years.

When they started talking about the house being too much for them and thinking about selling it, Mrs. Glover and her husband got the idea to buy it and turn it into a bed and breakfast. They were tired of living in a big city, so he quit his job at General Motors and they moved to Hideaway. They both took jobs in town, he at the bank and she at the school, and made the home their pet project. It was obvious that it was a true labor of love for them.

She showed Emily all through the house, sharing the details of all the work they had put into it. They stopped at a portrait of her grandparents in the study. Her grandmother had the same kind eyes as she did.

Mrs. Glover showed her through the kitchen and gave her permission to use whatever she wanted in order to pack a lunch for herself. Emily packed up some fruit and cheese and headed out for a long walk on the beach. She took her Bible and journal with her, hoping for some good time with God.

∞∞∞

She walked far enough that she got away from the crowds and found a perfect solitary place. She spread her blanket on the sand and pulled out her journal. "Well, here I am, Lord, in paradise. This place is beautiful and charming and peaceful and no one has recognized me. Can I please stay?"

After a while of writing about how much she loved the little town and reading in the Psalms, she pulled out her lunch. She wasn't sure how Mrs. Glover – Evelyn, as she had insisted on being called – had managed to do it, but she'd snuck a little note into the lunch bag.

"May you find what you're looking for, both on your walk on the beach today and always. God loves you and has a perfect plan for your life."

She then quoted Jeremiah 29:11, "For I know the plans I have for you," declares the Lord, "plans to prosper you and not to harm you, plans to give you hope and a future." It was one of the verses that Emily had been clinging to since her nightmare had begun back in LA.

"Well, that seems like enough confirmation to me, Lord. At least for now, I'm staying."

∞∞∞

By the time she got back to the bed and breakfast, she was more than ready for a bath. She didn't realize how far she had walked and forgot that walking on sand was such a workout. After gladly accepting the Epsom salt and private bathtub Evelyn offered, she went to revel in her newfound peace.

She was feeling relaxed for the first time in months as she laid in the bathtub until the hot water became room temperature. She was again thankful for the little bit of money she had set aside for such a time as this. It would be enough to pay for a couple of months' rent and groceries while she figured out what to do next.

What to do next was a big question. Thanks to Colin, she had no career left. His sins cast a long shadow, and the studio was quick to terminate her employment along with his when he was exposed as the predator he was. Since her recent work experience had all been in the entertainment industry, it would be of little use to her now.

Her name was mud. *Actually, Mrs. Mud. I'm once removed. About to be fully removed.*

She couldn't wait to not be his Mrs. anymore. It was going to be great to be Emily Spencer again.

Working as a producer on a home makeover show gave her a wide variety of skills, but she wasn't sure how they would apply to real life in a small town. She wondered if anyone in the greater Hideaway area was looking for someone to juggle budgets, schedule and manage multiple construction and decorating crews, and peel diva designers off the ceiling when necessary. She was very good at her job, but those skills didn't necessarily apply to every job market.

Maybe she would apply for a job at the cute furniture store in town. Judging by the displays in the front windows, whoever owned that knew a thing or two about design. She quickly realized that may work against her and her heart sank. If they watched design shows, they may have heard about Colin's activities and have the same impression about her part in it that the rest of the industry had. *If only he could have had self-control. If only I would have had eyes to see what he was doing and see through his lies.*

"How did I miss it, Lord? I knew those women. I worked with them. Why didn't they feel comfortable telling me what was going on? I would have helped them."

She started crying. Again. She knew it wasn't true. They could see that she was blind to the real Colin and that she was clinging to that blindness. She couldn't help them because she couldn't see the need.

Time to get back into therapy, Emily. Well past time, to be honest. She didn't want to open up any cans of emotional worms before leaving town, so she'd put that off. She added it to her to-do list.

Chapter 6

Emily was shocked at how much she had accomplished in the 24 hours since she had decided to make Hideaway her home. Since the summer season had wound down and fall was less busy, Evelyn was happy to allow her to rent the small room in exchange for utilities plus help around the house. It was apparently pretty hard to find good cleaning people in town and Evelyn had recently lost the help she had.

There was a lot of fall cleanup work to be done and Evelyn shared with her that she had more rooms that she used to rent out, but she'd had to scale back when the upkeep became too much. If Emily wanted to work on getting the other rooms back in order, she could have a place to stay for cheap for as long as she wanted.

It was an ideal arrangement. Emily had learned a lot about how to make an old place come alive on a tight budget when she worked on the shows. She was confident that she could help out and could still have time to find other work to get her by.

Housing: Check.

With two weeks to go before her name change back to her maiden name would be official and legal, she couldn't do much in the way of applying for a job. She decided that for the time being, she would go back to where she started and find some small businesses that needed accounting work done. Most of her work could be done online, so she wouldn't be limited by the geography in Northern Michigan.

Her dad had already offered to throw some work her way. He always said she was the only one he trusted with his books, so they called it a win-win.

Immediate income: check.

A few quick texts with Simone, her therapist in LA, was all it took to schedule a phone session.

Mental health: forthcoming.

She walked over to the red brick post office and made arrangements to get a P.O. Box. Going to the post office to get her mail might seem less quaint in the winter, but for now it felt very special.

Communication with outside world: check.

She even called her attorney's office and gave them her new contact information and got an update on both the criminal case and her divorce. After her attorney, Janice Strickland, gave Emily the pertinent information, her secretary of the week, Tiffany Something-or-Other, came back on the line to give her version of updating, which was basically a summary of social media and local gossip shows.

Emily pretended to lose the signal and hung up. Being in a small town in the middle of nowhere had its advantages. *Maybe Simone can help me get my conflict resolution skills out of seventh grade.*

Boundaries: lacking.

As she walked back toward the Shoreside Inn, the ringtone told her in crass but uncertain terms that Colin was calling. "Sorry, pal. Small town, big hills. No signal!" She smiled to herself as she silenced the ringer and went on her way. *I do love ringtones. Maybe I really am in seventh grade and this is all a dream. If that's true, I need to have better dreams.*

Boundaries: not as bad as I thought.

She looked down at the lake and decided she needed another beach fix before returning to the B and B. After thinking about making some calls, she realized she didn't really want to talk to anyone or have anyone to talk to anyway. She had spoken to her parents earlier and told them about the picturesque little town and about her plans. They tried to be supportive even though they didn't understand her need to go so far away from both her childhood and recent homes. She turned her phone off and her attention to the waves.

Chapter 7

T here was that familiar smell of bacon again. That smell would never get old. She had been in Hideaway for four weeks and still loved smelling bacon and coffee as she woke up.

Emily washed her face, put on some clothes, and walked downstairs. There were three middle-aged ladies sitting in the dining room finishing their breakfasts. They were on their way to a women's retreat and had driven up from Illinois the night before.

"Good morning, ladies."

She was enjoying having people to talk to in the mornings. When she was back in LA, she had convinced herself that she loved the solitude of being alone in the morning. Actually, she just loved not having Colin home. While that thought had initially made her sad, and frankly a little guilty, now she was starting to look at it as evidence that she was getting signals that something was wrong in her marriage – and in her husband – and that she was responding as any normal person would.

She began her day as was becoming her custom: breakfast and chatting with the guests, kitchen clean up with Evelyn, time at the library using the internet and either working or looking for ways to find clients, then back for lunch and work on the B and B in the afternoon when it was unlikely to be populated by guests.

The lawn was looking nice and the sign looked much perkier

with its fresh coat of paint and lettering. Thankfully, she was able to find some stencils at the craft store the last time she was in Traverse City. She wanted the sign to look like it was painted by an adult, even if it didn't look like it was painted by an artist. Looking at the finished product, she had to admit it looked good.

It was a joy doing her part to help Evelyn with the house, and she was thrilled to be doing home improvements with no cameras or crew or diva designers or confused homeowners or controlling husbands around. The outside of the house was looking better and she was even making progress on the rooms that had been locked and forgotten.

Somehow with all that she was doing to improve the B and B, she had never run into Joe, the handyman everyone raved about. He seemed to stop by in the mornings when she was working at the library or in the evenings when she was watching the sunset. She was hoping to meet him soon because she had some questions for him about one of the rooms she was working on and didn't want to concern Evelyn. She would wait for the opportunity to get his opinion on the sly.

The last time she had seen buckling in flooring like that, the construction worker on set showed her the easy way to make it look better but warned her that it could be covering up a festering water problem that would come back to cost the homeowners a lot of money later. She had pleaded alongside him to fix it right for the homeowners, but Colin refused to go over budget and swore them to secrecy, then accused her of having an affair with the construction worker. He was off the set a week later. *Lucky guy.*

Judging by the quality of work she had seen by Joe, he would know what size problem it was and would be able to fix it. She just hoped it wouldn't break the bank – or his back. He was probably an old friend of Evelyn's. Maybe he was even sweet on her. That would explain why he didn't charge her. All Emily knew about him was that he was also widowed, he loved Evelyn's cooking, and that he was incredibly generous with his time.

Chapter 8

Now that she was several sessions into therapy, Emily was opening up more than she ever had. It was freeing to be so real and honest.

Truth be told, she was honest with Simone before, but not with herself. The freedom was coming with finally being honest with herself first, then sharing it with Simone.

She was seeing that she had denied all of Colin's character deficiencies as a defense mechanism. By the time she realized he wasn't the perfect husband she thought he would be, or even a standard good one, she had no one to turn to for support. He had seen to that.

When they met, he had swept her off her feet. He wined and dined her, catered to her every whim, and took up all of her free time. He was like her own fairy tale prince who stepped off the pages of a book. When she saw things that bothered her, like the way he treated wait staff and valets, she explained it away as him being tired or distracted.

When he offered her a job on the show he was executive producing, it seemed like the perfect solution to them wanting to spend more time together. He had said she would be perfect for the job because of her organizational skills and ability to soothe people when needed. Dramatic designers and nervous homeowners needed soothing pretty often, and she was up to the task. Unfortunately, executive producers needed soothing too, and her job didn't end at the close of the workday.

Before she knew it, Colin was her entire world. No wonder it was too much to admit to herself that she had married a narcissist and that the marriage didn't mean the same thing to him that it did to her. No wonder people assumed that she knew about his extracurricular activities. *Little did they know. I didn't even know when he took it upon himself to sneak off and get a vasectomy while we were supposedly trying to start a family. And when I found out, I latched on to his rationalization that he did it because it would be too hard on* me *to have children and reach* 'my' *career goals and dreams.*

She was still having a hard time with the guilt about the women he had victimized and couldn't get past how she could have missed it. Many of those women were her friends, or at least friendly acquaintances. They were women she cared about.

Simone was kind but firm as she reminded Emily that she was not responsible for his behavior.

"I was responsible for his schedule, his home, his show, and his vacations. I was convinced that I was responsible for his moods, his success, his happiness . . . I guess it's just a logical jump that I was responsible for his actions too.

"It's starting to sink in that I couldn't be responsible for things I didn't know were going on." She laughed. "Suddenly the idea that this was somehow my fault is starting to sound absurd."

"Eureka!" They laughed together.

It felt great to laugh. It felt great to let Colin be responsible for Colin. Though it was painful, it felt good to take responsibility for herself, too. If she could make bad decisions and sleepwalk through life, she could wake up and make good ones. She could make good decisions for *herself*. What a concept.

Chapter 9

W hen she received the final divorce decree, she felt a mix of relief and sorrow. She spent most of that day at her favorite private spot on the beach processing it all.

When Colin finally stopped cajoling and begging her to come back, it was like a switch had flipped. He went into full vindictive mode and made all sorts of accusations about Emily marrying him for his money and ability to further her career at the network.

She didn't really care about that. People who knew her knew it wasn't true, and people who were around when they first met saw how he pursued her and she adored him. The only thing that he said that bothered her was about her work on the show. He claimed that others thought she was incompetent but he saved her job. *What a hero. What a putz.*

She had written out her own affidavit about both their personal and working relationship. Her lawyer had made a great argument about how he had caused her to lose her job and found several others who worked on the show who vouched for her professionalism and competence. It touched her that they stepped up on her behalf.

The judge was touched too, and despite Colin's attempts to freeze her out, ordered a settlement amount that, while not huge, would give her a safety net while she rebuilt her life. Most of

Colin's money was gone, or soon would be, thanks to the loss of his job and the lawsuits by the women whose lives he had destroyed. Emily had offered to testify on behalf of any of the women who thought it would be helpful.

As she sat on the beach, she cried about the loss of her hopes for marriage, about the loss of the life she thought she had, about the loss of friends as her world became consumed by him, and about the loss of trust in herself. It felt good to cry it out.

She had started to reconnect with some of the people she had fallen out of touch with, the relationships that had been casualties of her marriage. They were all surprisingly forgiving and it felt good to repair those bridges.

When she returned to the Shoreside Inn, there was a beautiful vase filled with fresh fall flowers from the garden and a note from Evelyn. She had been nothing but supportive when Emily tearfully spilled her story out a couple of weeks before. She must have guessed what was in the envelope that had arrived that morning.

Emily took a nice long bath and talked to God about her future. She was finally starting to believe that she had one, that it was *okay* to have one. The envelope on the dresser was the tangible evidence that her old life was officially over.

Chapter 10

The early October air had a welcome chill. She had missed fall when she lived in California. She was glad she had found a couple of resale shops in Traverse City and had begun stocking up on warmer clothes. The new-to-her sweater and skirt she had found were perfect for the time of year. The sweater was a thick cream-colored cable knit and made her feel cozy, like she was walking around with a blanket draped over her shoulders. The straight long brown skirt balanced the bulkiness of the sweater nicely and the suede boots were the perfect finishing touch. She didn't know why she was so nervous – she was just going to church.

She had been putting off walking into the old white church that had first beckoned her. At first, she preferred her Sunday mornings in her tiny room with her coffee, Bible, journal, podcasts from a few churches she followed online, and plenty of Kleenex. She felt too raw to meet new people and avoid questions.

Now that she was healing and her new life was off and running, it was time. Evelyn had given her an open invitation to join her and today was the day she finally accepted. When they walked toward the church, it felt like coming home. She desperately hoped it would meet her admittedly lofty expectations.

There was such a feeling of community there. From the moment she stepped through the door into the small foyer, she could sense it. The twin wooden staircases on either side of the foyer that went up to the sanctuary seemed to invite any who entered to be a part of the church family.

She recognized a few faces from around town. Evelyn's bridge club ladies were there, as were a few ladies from her book club. Ben from the post office was there, as was Rachel from the library and Pam from the grocery store. Everyone greeted her warmly and welcomed her.

She followed Evelyn up the creaky stairs to the sanctuary, where the wood pews gleamed in the sun that was shining through the stained glass windows. The Tiffany lamps coordinated nicely with the windows.

As the music of the organ filled the room, Emily exhaled. It felt good to be in a church that didn't look like a high school gym or a theater. This church felt like home.

∞∞∞

When the pastor asked everyone to greet those around them after the opening hymn, she was met with many outstretched hands and warm welcomes. As she turned to greet the people in the row behind her, her breath caught.

The man with the outstretched hand had the most beautiful blue eyes she had ever seen. They were almost cobalt, framed by his brown locks and strong jaw. He gripped her hand firmly and smiled as he greeted her. She was pretty sure she just stared. She hoped she didn't drool.

He was the kind of handsome that one didn't look directly at, like a solar eclipse. Not the photoshopped or LA type of hand-some – *better*. He was the rugged and *real* type of handsome.

The gentleman to his right had the same blue eyes and warm smile as he reached for her hand and welcomed her. Thankfully, the pastor cajoled people into taking their seats quickly. *Saved by announcements and prayer requests.*

She reminded herself that she wasn't there to meet men and that her days of romance were gone. At minimum, they were on hold for a very long time. Still, she couldn't help but be hyper-aware of his presence behind her. It took a lot of prayer to focus back on the pastor.

The rest of the service met and exceeded her expectations. They sang some of the few hymns she knew and the pastor talked about the story of John the Baptist's parents, which just happened to be one of her favorites.

She always got chills when it got to the part where his father, Zechariah, who was unable to speak after doubting God's proc-lamation that he would have a son, wrote on a tablet, "His name is John" and had his speech restored. Such a beautiful picture of God's redemption, it reminded her that He was restoring her, too.

She excused herself after the service, skipping the fellowship time that she wasn't quite ready for, and walked back to the B and B. Her new boots were less than ideal for the walk, but she enjoyed smelling the fresh air and leaves burning in the distance.

Chapter 11

S
he suddenly had the desire to make chili. Fall weather always had that effect on her. She exchanged her skirt and
boots for jeans and slippers and headed to the kitchen.
One of the benefits of living with someone who knew just about
everyone in town was having a kitchen stocked with fresh vege-
tables and grass-fed meat from the locals. She started the meat
browning, grabbed a jar of recently canned tomatoes, and got to
work.

Thankfully, Chef Google helped her find a recipe that she could
make even with her dusty kitchen skills. She hummed the hymns
from earlier while she chopped and measured. She was enjoying
getting back to cooking and had a new appreciation for fresh,
local ingredients.

Evelyn offered to help when she returned, but Emily was just
about finished. As she was on her way to take a nap, Evelyn men-
tioned that Joe would be coming for dinner.

"Great, I can finally meet the mysterious handyman!" *And
maybe arrange for a little romance between him and the lady of the
house while I'm at it.* Even though she wasn't looking for romance
herself, she could sure help Evelyn find some.

Since they were having company and the quickest way to a
man's heart was supposedly through his stomach, Emily decided
to make a slightly bigger event out of dinner than she had origin-
ally planned. She found Evelyn's old recipe tin and made her apple

pie. When she took inventory of the salad fixings available, she was happy to find a fresh loaf of bread from the bakery down the street. They had everything for a tasty fall meal.

She had thought about how she could slip her number to Joe so they could talk privately about the flooring issue, then thought better of it when she realized that his hearing might be even worse than Evelyn's. This was going to need to be a face to face conversation. It might be a bit tricky to pull that off without her knowing, so she made up another question about some crown molding in the bedroom in question. That would give her an excuse to get him alone and show him the potential damage.

Once everything was prepared, she decided to take her own nap. She was going to have to be fully alert to pull off getting Joe alone to discuss the flooring, setting the stage for senior romance, and then excusing herself so that nature could take its course.

Chapter 12

When Emily came back downstairs, Evelyn was setting the table for dinner. She had changed into more casual clothes, but still looked very stylish. She was the kind of lady Emily aspired to be – always gracious, quick to help others, a positive attitude no matter what was going on, and a fashion sense that didn't stop when she hit sixty.

"Joe is fixing that chandelier that keeps flickering, then we'll eat, if that's okay with you. I see you made a pie and it smells delicious! It's Joe's favorite, too, and I always make him at least one apple pie in the fall."

Emily was sure she saw a twinkle in Evelyn's eye when she talked about Joe. She internally patted herself on the back and called herself brilliant for setting up a romantic dinner. It was obvious she truly cared about the man. She went to find some candles, using the excuse that when the weather gets cold, the candles come out. *I'm a matchmaking genius!*

∞∞∞

When she walked back into the dining room, she almost walked right into a back attached to a pair of broad shoulders. When he turned around, she saw that it was Mr. Eclipse from church. *Oh! Why is he here? Don't look directly at him! Try not to stare or drool this time!*

"There you are," Evelyn began. "Joe, this is Emily, the house-guest I was telling you about."

Chapter 13

*T*his is Joe? You've got to be kidding me, Lord. She shook his outstretched hand and hoped he didn't notice her flushing. She tried to manage a polite smile and casual tone. "Nice to finally meet you, Joe. I'm a big fan of your work."

That sounded so LA.

She spent the meal focusing on diverting the conversation to the others and avoiding looking directly at Mr. Eclipse. She was not looking for a relationship, but she was only human, after all. It had been a very long time since she had felt this way just being near a man.

As soon as she could do so without being rude, she made an excuse to get up from the table and began cleaning up in the kitchen.

What is wrong with you, Emily? He's just a man. Men are bad. Just stay away from him and you'll be fine. She scrubbed harder than necessary on the stove top.

She heard someone come through the swinging door from the dining room.

"Can I help?" Joe. *Come on, Lord. Please give me a break with this guy. I can only take so much.*

"No, I've got it covered. With all you do around here, the least we can do is give you a meal that you don't have to clean up after."

"Okay, well thank you for the delicious dinner. And that pie was fantastic! It's one of my favorite parts of fall."

"The rest of it is on that pie plate for you. Evelyn says it's tradition for you to take it home."

She kept scrubbing too hard on the kitchen appliances and anything she could get her hands on – anything to avoid looking at him.

He thanked her again and excused himself. She chastised herself for the knot in her stomach and disappointment when he left the room.

As she heard the front door close behind him, she realized that she completely forgot about the flooring problem. She smacked her hand to her forehead. *Doh!*

Chapter 14

Joe Callahan walked the three blocks to his house with a spring in his step that he tried to convince himself was due to the apple pie in his hand. While it was true that he would likely finish the pie by nightfall, he knew that wasn't the only thing making his feet feel light.

Stop it, Callahan. You don't need to be thinking about a woman. That's not a part of your life anymore.

He strode into the kitchen, set the pie down, and walked right back out to his truck. There was nothing like a hard night's work to get his mind off things he shouldn't be thinking about. He didn't usually work on Sundays, but since his daughter Lily was with her grandparents for the night and he needed a distraction, he headed out to the house he was renovating to flip.

The place was a mess when he bought it in the spring. The previous owners were a family well-known for arguing and suing each other, so when the matriarch died, her children fought for three years over who would get the property. During that time no one allowed any of the others access, so no one knew about the pipes bursting.

When the damage was discovered, it was too much for the 'winner' of the family brawl to take care of and he ended up selling it to Joe for pennies on the dollar. He had suggested to Joe that he should just level it and start over, but the big, old, Craftsman house had great bones and Joe was determined to restore it to its former glory. He remembered how beautiful it was when he played there as a kid, before the family turned on each other.

Joe had made a startling amount of progress in the few months he'd had it. He had torn out the damaged pipes, floorboards, and plaster to make sure there was no mold anywhere, replaced the roof and several boards on the siding, and had started on the electrical.

The electrical job was going to be bigger than he felt competent to do, so he had made arrangements to barter services with a friend who was a master electrician. He was slightly ahead of schedule, which made him breathe a sigh of relief. He wanted to make sure the exterior was all fixed before winter hit, and in Summit County, winter could hit at any time.

∞∞∞

Just as he was wondering when Randy might be able to work on the wiring, he heard a truck outside.

"Well, speak of the devil! I was just wondering when you were going to have time to come over here."

"I was on my way home and saw your truck in the driveway. I have a few hours now and we've got some daylight left, so how about if you stop talking and help me get my tools out of the truck?" The old friends laughed and got to work.

Joe was always happy to act as assistant to people who knew more than him; it was like a self-study apprentice program. Everything he had learned about home repair and renovation had come from doing the grunt work and watching others who knew what they were doing.

Chapter 15

E mily decided she needed a break, and didn't care that it was only ten a.m. The budget she was working on was exhausting. It was like trying to put a five hundred piece puzzle together and make it look like a complete picture with only four hundred seventy-five pieces. She had forgotten that sometimes bookkeeping clients expected her to be a miracle worker.

The few clients she'd found were helping with the finances, but not quite enough to support herself without dipping into the money from the divorce settlement. She was trying to avoid that as much as possible and wanted to use it as her retirement savings. Even though she had been able to manage better than she thought she could, every once in a while she had to take out a few dollars to make ends meet.

Between the bookkeeping puzzle and thinking about the shock of the dinner guest a couple nights before, she was fighting a losing battle with her ability to concentrate.

She decided some manual labor would be a great way to give herself a break while still feeling productive, and put on her work clothes. Sanding a floor should be a great release, and even a workout. It would also give her a baseline for what the floor looked like so that when she got up the nerve to be in the same room with Joe without acting like a teenage girl, she could describe the changes she was seeing. She wondered if he went to First Community Church regularly and if he would be there again on Sunday. Just as she was chastising herself again for thinking of him again, she walked into the room and gasped.

"Oh no! It's worse!" There was no putting off talking to Joe now. Evelyn was in Traverse City for the next few hours, so this would be a perfect time to have him take a look at it if he was free.

His number was in Evelyn's address book and Emily called right away. She was relieved when he didn't answer, and convinced herself that the message she left sounded coherent. She started moving things around in the room as much as possible to expose the floor and heard a voice downstairs.

"Hello? It's Joe Callahan. I got your message. It sounded urgent, so I headed right over."

"Up here, Joe. This is the room with the problem." Her breathlessness and pounding heart were definitely because she was moving furniture. *Definitely.*

He took one look at it and stifled what was probably a word he avoided saying in front of ladies. "When did this start?"

"I'm not sure. It was a tiny bit uneven a few weeks ago and I was planning on telling you about it, but today I walked in and saw this buckling."

"Do you know where the water shut off valve for the house is? This is fresh, so something is leaking right now. We've got to stop it before this house looks like mine."

He looked like he thought better of it. "Actually, we don't have time to waste and I know where the valve is, so I'll go shut off the water. Can you keep moving stuff out of this room? And grab some towels just in case."

He left the room and she exhaled. Well, at least now she had a distraction from his eyes.

"Lord, if we're going to be working in close quarters, I'm going to need You to intervene. Can you please make him look like a lizard person or something?"

Chapter 16

Joe made his way through the basement to the main water shut off valve, glad for an excuse to get out of that bedroom. That was way too close. Something about her holey jeans and old Michigan sweatshirt was a little too much to ignore. She had even picked the right school.

Button it up, Callahan.

He shut off the water, called a friend who was adept at plumbing emergencies, and started back upstairs. Mitch said he would be there in ten minutes.

Only ten minutes of alone time with the temptress. I can do all things through Him who gives me strength. I can do all things through Him who gives me strength.

He ran out to his truck to grab the rest of his tools. That would burn up a few minutes. Maybe his willpower could fill up a bit in that time. Somehow it seemed to be in short supply when he was around her. His guilt threatened to overwhelm him and he focused on getting his tools in order.

Chapter 17

By the time Joe and Mitch found and repaired the source of the leak, it was after one. The good news was that it was a fairly simple fix. The bad news was that it was only a temporary fix. Making it right was going to be a big job, as was fixing the floor that had been damaged.

So much for not worrying Evelyn.

Emily volunteered to go make lunch since her skill set was not quite up to theirs in the plumbing department. It felt good to help as much as she did and she reveled in their surprise at how useful she was. They had finally stopped trying to describe tools and just named what they were looking for when they realized this was not her first home repair.

Just as she started heading back upstairs with the sandwiches she had made, Evelyn walked in the front door. Emily gave the briefest and least expensive-sounding explanation she could think of for what was going on in her house and continued upstairs. Evelyn followed.

Emily was relieved to see that Joe and Mitch were as committed to not worrying her as she was. They were both really decent men. *That doesn't help my situation here, Lord. Can't you give him a flaw?*

Mitch approached her with a sheepish look on his face. "Would you think me rude if I took the sandwich to go? I need to get back to the hardware store and relieve my nephew. It's a little much for him to be there alone."

"That's no problem. Thank you for coming over as quickly as you did and for staying so long." She smiled.

He smiled back with a nice, non-threatening smile that didn't make her knees go weak – just the kind she liked on a handsome, single man these days.

He hugged Evelyn as he made his way toward the door. "We'll get this place fixed up good as new, Evelyn. Don't you worry about a thing. Thank you again for lunch, Emily. It was nice meeting you."

"You too, Mitch." She watched him go and realized the only thing between her and Joe was about two and a half feet and Evelyn.

Chapter 18

The initial fix at Evelyn's took less time than they thought it would. That was a relief to Joe. After he had eaten quickly and made sure that everything was stable, he practically ran to his truck. He couldn't get out of there fast enough.

He had a feeling that Emily didn't want to spend time with him any more than he wanted to spend time with her. She had different reasons, obviously. He wasn't sure what he had done to offend her, but she avoided him as much as she could. She even avoided looking at him or talking to him when they were working together. Sure, she was helpful and polite, but it seemed obvious that she was saying the least amount possible. She was definitely more relaxed with Mitch and seemed to have an easier rapport with him. He made a mental note to ask Mitch if he had heard him say anything out of line.

For his part, he was avoiding her, too. He was noticing her big green eyes and full lips on a regular basis, and that was not helpful. He wondered what it would be like to kiss those lips, then he felt like a rotten adulterer for thinking about it.

The Rolling Stones started playing on his phone, alerting him to a call from his mother. *Saved by the bell.*

"Hi, Mom. I'm just finishing up at Evelyn's. Is Lily ready to be picked up?"

"Well actually, I was wondering if we could keep her for a while longer and if you would like to join us for dinner. She started her nap a little late, so she's still sleeping now. She wants to have a princess tea party and I want to have burgers one more time before Dad puts the grill away for the winter. I thought that might give you a few hours to work on the house, too.

"That sounds perfect. I'll aim for six." *A few more hours of manual labor should be enough to clear my head.*

"See you then."

He hung up the phone, feeling thankful that Lily had such amazing grandparents. He didn't know how he would be able to raise her without all their help. She seemed pretty well-adjusted for a girl who never knew her mother.

Chapter 19

E mily was exhausted from the hours spent hunched over her laptop. She was still sore from the construction project from a couple of days before and sitting in an awkward position didn't help.

As she was about to go take a soothing bath, she saw the certified letter that Evelyn had slid under her door while she was working. She wasn't expecting anything, and since the troubles with Colin started, she had come to dread anything that looked official. It usually meant bad news, so she braced herself.

The return address showed her attorney's office. The first page was a handwritten note from Janice.

> **Surprise!**
>
> **All the jewelry that we thought Colin pawned was safely hidden in a safe deposit box in BOTH OF YOUR NAMES. You know what that means.**
>
> **Attached is the invoice as well as pictures of the items. We'll be happy to ship what you want to you and sell the rest, if that's what you still want.**
>
> **J.**

She let out a little yelp. The timing couldn't be more perfect. There wasn't much jewelry, but it would easily cover the cost of the repairs that had just taken up their day at the B and B.

She started to call Joe to discuss how much he wanted and ask him to let her pay it without Evelyn knowing, then felt the knot in her stomach. She called Mitch at the hardware store instead.

Mitch told her she would need to talk to Joe about the cost of his materials and labor, but gave her his own portion of both. It was a shockingly low number. She knew that was probably not covering materials and his cost for paying someone to run the hardware store while he was away. Evelyn sure had an effect on people.

Chapter 20

J oe looked around the living room, beaming; he felt like a proud father. The hardwood floor looked great. He still had a lot of repairs to do on the plaster, and the molding was going to take a bit of time this winter, but he took a moment to savor the most recent task finished.

He wished he could keep the place. He had loved the house forever and had enjoyed the repairs on this more than any house he had flipped. Lily was content in their small bungalow, but he would love to see her in a big living room like this.

For a brief second, he pictured her playing on this floor. Her little table would fit perfectly in the indented area in the corner where there used to be a large built-in buffet. He imagined her having her beloved tea parties with her brothers and sisters. *Whoa, where did that come from? You've got to stop inhaling the fumes here, bro.*

He tried to shake the image from his head. Lily wasn't going to be *having* brothers and sisters, and there was no use dwelling on dreams that died along with her mother.

Joe and Janie had talked about having a house full of kids. Lily was supposed to be the *first* child, not the *only* child. That was when they thought they would grow old together.

Neither of them imagined that things would go so horribly wrong on the happiest day of their lives.

His mind flashed back to that day. Labor was going along as it was supposed to, according to the nurse and Janie was a trooper. He hated to see her in pain, but she was brave.

When all of a sudden she went from squeezing his hand so hard through a contraction that he teased her about breaking bones to going limp and losing consciousness, he didn't know what was happening. When they wheeled her out of the birthing room he had no idea that he would never see her alive again.

He shook his head again. He needed the beach, just for a moment. It was the place he could always get solace when memories got the best of him. Even though it was getting chilly, he drove with the windows down. It was obvious that he needed some oxygen.

Chapter 21

Emily was freezing. She wrapped her blanket around herself more tightly as she reminded herself that she needed to get back into the swing of dressing for cold weather. If she was going to continue to make a nightly habit of watching the sunset, she would eventually have to enjoy the view from her car, but she wasn't ready for that yet.

Sipping her hot chocolate from the insulated cup, she savored the warm liquid in her throat. She hoped that if she focused hard enough on it, she would feel warm all over.

She looked up and saw a familiar looking figure walking toward the water. *Joe. Great, now I can't even escape him at the beach.*

He looked tormented. *I guess I'm not the only one who needs Vitamin Beach regularly.* She watched him sit on the shore and stare out at the lake. At times he looked like he was talking to someone on his Bluetooth, at others his head hung low.

She wanted to go over and put her arm around his broad shoulders to comfort him. *No boys, Emily. They're bad news.* Still, she couldn't help but watch him. He looked so vulnerable.

She finally tore her eyes away from him when it looked like he was heading back in her direction and she pretended to read the Bible in her hands. *There's got to be a special place in hell for people who use a Bible as a prop.*

"Sorry, Lord. It's an emergency."

At just the right – or maybe wrong – time, she looked up and their eyes locked. She felt a jolt and thought it was a small earthquake. When she remembered that they didn't have those in Northern Michigan, she convinced herself she was shivering from the cold.

"Hey, Joe, I didn't realize that was you." *Liar.*

"Hi, Emily. Are you as cold as you look?"

"Colder." She pulled her blanket closer.

"The sunset is worth it though, huh?" *He looks as uncomfortable talking to me as I feel talking to him.*

"Absolutely. Hey, do you have a minute? I wanted to talk to you about your bill for Evelyn's place. I'm about to come into some money that I think should cover your expenses and labor and I'd like to pay it for her."

He stared at her for a long minute. His eyes darkened and he looked like she had just told him she kicked puppies for fun.

"I don't charge Evelyn." He spat the words and stormed away before she could say anything else.

"Well, Lord. You showed me that he has a flaw. He's cranky." Immediately she knew that wasn't true. She'd just watched him have what appeared to be a difficult conversation, to say the least, and it was obvious by his reddened eyes that he had been crying. She instantly regretted her timing and she kicked herself for being so oblivious. Even if he wasn't already upset, she'd offended him by trying to pay him for something he did out of love.

How LA of you.

Chapter 22

*W*ho does she think she is, offering to pay me for helping my own friend? That woman is like family to me and this chick – this stranger – thinks she can pay me? That's a lot of nerve. And what was that about being about to come into some money? Nervy and pretentious!

He'd heard she moved from LA. *Apparently they don't help friends out there.*

He took the long way home, hoping the drive would give him time to get control of his mood and attitude. It helped, but one look at the tiny blonde running toward him as he walked through his front door went a long way toward that end. Lily was wearing her favorite princess night gown and was very obviously trying to show off her hands. He scooped her up, careful not to smudge the nails she was so proud of.

"How's my little princess? You look extra beautiful tonight, Your Highness. Have you had fun with Grandma and Grandpa today?"

"We painted naiws, Daddy! Look at my pretty naiws. They're *pink!*"

"I see that! What a beautiful pink they are." He kissed her cheek as he carried her over into the living room, where Mary, Janie's mother, was beaming.

"Hi, Mom." He kissed her cheek. "You did a great job on her nails, as usual."

"We had a fun day today, didn't we sweetheart?"

Lily grinned and buried her face in her daddy's neck.

"Lily, can you go ask Grandpa to read your story to you? Daddy and I will be right in."

She scampered down the hall, calling for her grandpa, and Joe turned to face Mary. She was looking very serious all of a sudden and fumbled with a tissue in her hand.

"Joe, I've been thinking about you and Lily a lot lately – well, you know I always think about you, but the Lord has put something on my heart that I have to say. Sit with me, will you?"

"Of course." He sat on the couch next to her.

"You know I love you and you know I loved my daughter."

"Yes, and I love you too. What is it you need to say?"

She took a deep breath. "Joe, God says it's not good for man to be alone. And I say it's not good for a little girl to not have a mother. I know you loved my Janie with all of your heart. I know you would have given anything to save her life and that you would give anything to bring her back." She dabbed at her eyes. "I'm not going to start pressuring you to start dating, but I just want you to know that we hope you find love again. We *want* you to find love again. It's been *two and a half years,* Joe. You were a wonderful husband to our little girl, and we want you to be happy again. Janie would want you to be happy again, and she would want her little girl to have a mommy. That's all I have to say, and now I just need a minute to cry."

Joe held her tightly and they took a minute to cry together.

"Thanks, Mom. I'm not really looking or sure how to look, but it means the world to me that you wouldn't see that as a betrayal of Janie. She will always be my first love and Lily's mom. She will never leave my heart." He pushed himself to continue. "But you're right. I can't avoid the possibility forever. It's not fair to Lily or to me. Or to Janie. I thought I was avoiding women because of Lily, but it's partly because I never want to hurt like that again."

"Loneliness is just another kind of hurt, son."

He gave her one last squeeze. "Do you have any more of those tissues? I have something in my eye." He attempted a wink.

Chapter 23

Emily was sure one of these houses was the one that Joe was working on. She spied his truck and slowly pulled into the driveway behind it. She took a few deep breaths and asked God to untie the knot in her stomach. It had taken a few days to work up the courage to go talk to him, and she was determined to do it, stomach knot and all.

She was about to knock when she caught sight of him. *Whoa, even when he's mad at me he's way too hot for me to talk to like a normal person. Deep breath, girl. Use your words. You're not here for romance. You're here to make things right.*

Just then he looked up and motioned her in. They both spoke at the same time, offering apologies for the conversation at the beach.

"Wait. Ladies first. Please."

"Okay, if you insist. Go ahead."

"I didn't mean to overstep or to give the impression that you're all about the money with Evelyn. I just wanted to help her and with all you do for her, I wanted to help you, too. I'm really sorry if I offended you."

"There's no apology needed, but I accept. And there's no excuse for the way I reacted that night. Evelyn is very special to me and helped me get through the hardest time in my life." He took a deep breath as if he needed a moment before going on. "The thought that I would expect payment for what I do for her just rubbed me the wrong way that night. I was in a foul mood after just arguing with God on the beach about some things and I shouldn't have engaged in any type of human contact. So please accept *my* apology."

"Of course I accept." She breathed a sigh of relief and smiled at him. "Wow, that was easier than I thought. At the risk of being very 1950, I brought some pie for you. I thought I might need to work harder for your forgiveness."

"Darn it, I should have held out a little more! Do I still get to keep the pie even though I caved so quickly?"

She laughed. "Of course!"

He went to the kitchen and found some forks. He gestured toward the built-in storage shelves lining the wall since there was no other seating in the empty room.

The knot in her stomach reappeared as she sat down. She wished the shelves were a little longer so she didn't have to sit quite so close to him – she also wished that she didn't want to sit even closer. She looked away from him as she attempted to regain her composure. At that moment she noticed the details of the room they were in.

"Wow, it's beautiful in here! I love all the different woods you used. I see cherry, oak, and maple, but what is this?"

"You know your woods. This is pine. I like to combine woods when I can. It makes it feel less like a showroom and more like a home."

He turned this gaze back to her. "Have you worked in renovating or construction before? I couldn't help but notice last week that you know your way around a tool box. And most people wouldn't have known that the amount of buckling you saw on Evelyn's floor was a sign of something serious."

"I used to have a job where I did a little bit of all of that. I really loved the actual work and creativity of it. It was fun to see something go from old and run down to fresh and vibrant. It was the production part that I hated." *Oops. Hopefully he didn't catch that.*

"Production part? Wait a minute, you moved here from LA, didn't you? Did you work on one of those home improvement shows?"

"Yes, a few of them."

"I knew you spoke the language. I watch some of those occasionally and I've gotten some good ideas from them. What brought you here?"

Did she dare? There was something so kind in his eyes. He wasn't acting all standoffish like usual and he was showing genuine interest.

I guess the pie really worked. You promised God and Simone that you would practice opening up. This is a good chance. If nothing else, it will chase this dangerous man away.

She took a deep breath and tried to control the shaking as she began to speak. "Are you familiar with the TV executive who was accused of sexual assault and workplace harassment? The one from a few months ago?"

"Do you mean that creep at the Home Improvement Channel?" His eyes went dark and filled with concern.

"Yes, that's the one. I'm Mrs. Creep. Well, I *was* Mrs. Creep. Now I'm Ex-Mrs. Creep." She waited for the accusing look, but only the look of concern remained.

"Wow. I'm stunned. Did you have any idea – sorry. It's none of my business. That must have been horrible."

She paused, absorbing her surprise at his compassion. "Thank you for not just assuming I knew and didn't care. Everyone in LA treated me like I was somehow in on it."

Tears stung her eyes but she looked directly at him. "I didn't know. I knew my husband was a self-absorbed jerk. I didn't know he was a predator."

"I'm sorry you had to go through all that. You seem to be handling it pretty well."

She smiled as she wiped her eye. "I'll pass your compliment on to my therapist. Jesus already heard you say it, so He got His credit. The two of them have been fixing me." They laughed easily.

This is nice ... maybe a little too nice.

He got a mischievous glint in his eye. "You probably shouldn't have told me all that, you know. Now that I've seen your work and know your experience, I'm going to be looking for your help as I finish that damaged floor next week and again this winter when I'm fixing things for Evelyn to get it ready for next summer. That place needs a bit of work, and it's best to do it when the guests are few and far between."

When he smiled, she felt like the entire room lit up.

That's it? Not even a subtle accusation? She relaxed a little bit and admitted it felt good to let out her secret. No, it felt *great*. After all, she was finally learning that it wasn't really *her* secret.

"Speaking of work, who are you fixing this place up for?"

"Sadly, the realtor. I've been flipping houses since my daughter was born. I started doing it full-time because I could work my schedule around taking care of her, and found out that I really love it. I'm usually happy to pass each place on so someone else can enjoy it, but this place is different. Maybe it's because I used to play here as a kid, or maybe it's because it's just such a beautiful place, but I'm having a hard time thinking about selling it. I keep picturing my daughter playing right there." He pointed to a corner of the room where there was a big cubby in the wall.

She pictured a little girl over there. "That would be a great place for tea parties."

He seemed to flinch.

He cleared his throat and stood suddenly. Was she imagining things, or did his eyes just get misty? Did she say something wrong again?

"Hey, sorry to keep you so long. You probably hoped to deliver pie, grovel, and get out. The sun is already setting. Don't you have an appointment at the beach?"

"How did you know?"

"The other night wasn't the first time I've seen you there at sunset." He offered a shy smile and took the pie plate into the kitchen.

$$\infty\infty\infty$$

The next Sunday she found herself looking for him as she entered the sanctuary. *Let's not start that. He's even more dangerous now that you know he's got a soft side.*

"Are you looking for someone, dear?"

"No, I'm just taking it all in." She smiled at Evelyn. The twinkle in her eye suggested she saw right through her. Emily forced her eyes to stay forward and to focus on the service.

Once again Pastor Ray talked about God showing His love and care for His people in unique ways. He used the story of the manna

SECOND CHANCE IN SUMMIT COUNTY

from heaven this time and pointed out that God always gives His children what they need, often in unconventional ways.

As he was talking, she thought about the "manna" she'd received recently – comfort after the demise of the miserable marriage she'd tried to save, a new life in a new town, a new friend in Evelyn, a tiny church that reminded her of God's love every week, reconnecting with friends from the past that she thought she'd lost forever, and a new level of honesty and courage. She had even spilled her whole story to her parents and apologized for hiding the truth about how miserable she had been for so long. Instead of reminding her that they had warned her not to marry Colin so quickly, as she expected, they just listened and told her how sorry they were for what she was going through.

Life was good for the first time in a long time. She let the tears flow down her cheeks. This time they were tears of gratitude.

Chapter 24

Joe packed his tools and supplies into his truck to go to Evelyn's house to work on the damaged floor. Now that the guests were mostly coming up only on weekends for fall color tours, he had more freedom to come in and work during the weekdays without bothering anyone.

Evelyn was in Traverse City for the day, so he planned to sneak in and tear out the rest of the floor boards that he wanted to replace while she was gone and before she tried to pay him or stop him. He was determined to restore the floor to the condition it was in before the water leak, whether Evelyn knew about it or not. Emily would be at the library, so he could focus on the job at hand without being distracted by her presence. He had found her presence even more distracting after getting to know her better and seeing more of who she was when they shared pie and apologies the week before. It was best to plan his visits to the Shoreside Inn for times when it was empty.

He thought back to the conversation he'd had with his father-in-law the previous afternoon. Bill had stopped by the flip house to offer help as Joe was tearing out the kitchen cabinets. He was a great help with demolition and they did their best Tim Allen impressions when they were destroying property. He wasn't usually one for a lot of words, so Joe knew to take what he said to heart when he did speak.

"Joe, Mary told me you two talked the other night. I'm glad

she had the courage to finally bring it up, because I didn't." He paused, as if pushing himself to say more. "One of the things that was important to me as the father of two little girls was to show them how fathers should treat their mothers and treat them. My father was terrible to my mother and I saw what it did to her, so I made it my job to give a proper example for my daughters. They both learned the lesson and married good men. I pray every night that someday you'll have the opportunity to show Lily the same thing." He paused again, and Joe swallowed hard.

Bill looked as if he had more to say, but he turned back to the cupboards and started back on the demo.

Joe pulled himself out of the memory and back into the present. An image of Emily in her holey jeans and sweatshirt came to mind.

"Lord, I don't know how to do this. I know they're right and that I need to be open to loving someone else, but just because I'm going to be open to love again doesn't mean that I need to do it with the first pretty girl to show up in town."

You know she's not just some pretty girl.

He squeezed the steering wheel hard.

"I need to focus on working today. Thank You for emptying that house so I can get some things done. Today is a good day to tear up floor boards – I could use a good sweat right about now."

He arrived at Evelyn's house and began unloading his supplies. As he walked in the front door, he heard music coming from upstairs. It was unusual to have music playing in an empty house, so he slowly crept up the stairs with his hammer in his hand in case he needed it.

He approached the bedroom as the music grew louder.

Emily was dancing as she carefully gathered floor boards to the beat and set them along the wall. He realized he was staring and smiling and that he'd better announce himself before he crossed a line and turned into a stalker.

"It looks like great minds think alike."

Chapter 25

Emily jumped. "How long have you been standing there?"

"Just long enough to see that you got to do all the fun stuff." He laughed as she felt herself flush. "I'm sorry. I didn't see your car and when I heard music, I thought I might have to take down a burglar."

"With a *hammer*?" Now they were both laughing.

He looked down at the inadequate weapon and shrugged. "It was already in my hand. I see you had the same idea as I had today. I also see that my timing is impeccable – you already got all of the boards that need replacing up."

"Well, now that I've done all the hard work, maybe you can help me carry these downstairs."

"I will if you don't tell Evelyn I was here."

"Why wouldn't you want her to know you were here?"

"She only lets me do repairs that absolutely have to be done. She's so concerned about taking advantage that she doesn't let me do everything that *needs* to be done and that I want to do. I planned to sneak in today and do this without her knowing so that she couldn't stop me."

His love for Evelyn filled her heart.

He's still a man, Emily. Don't get fooled.

"Well, I guess we'd better get the evidence out of here, then. The only problem is, we don't have wood to replace what just came out yet."

"It's in my truck."

∞∞∞

Emily was very aware of the close quarters they were in and tried to ignore the increased beat of her pulse. She was even more impressed with the quality of his work when she had an up-close view.

"Have you always been so precise? You take 'measure twice, cut once' to a whole new level."

"Blame that on my career in architecture in my former life. If things aren't exact, they don't fit. Getting it right the first time saves me work in the long run because I don't have to go back and redo anything later."

"Architecture, huh? Does it bother you to work on one room at a time instead of designing a whole house?"

"No, it's exactly the opposite. When I worked at the architecture firm, I was part of a team, so the jobs were divided up. I only worked on a part of the process and it made me crazy. That, and I hadn't earned the clout to have a say in the work I was doing or the finished product. That's why I like renovation jobs and flipping houses so much. I get to start at the beginning, make a plan, turn it into something special, and pass it off."

"But you said that's not the case with the house you're working on now."

"No, it's definitely not the case with that house." She was touched by how sad he looked.

"Is there any way you can keep it?"

"If there is, I haven't found it. I can't risk my daughter's future by overextending my finances. I try to carefully plan out when I'm purchasing, when I'm renovating, and when I'm selling, so that the finances stay even. Unless something changes over the months it's going to take to finish it, I'll be saying goodbye to it in the spring." He paused and put an optimistic smile on his face. "It's okay. There will be other houses. Someday I'll be able to give Lily a big living room to hold tea parties in."

"She sounds like a special girl." She smiled in his direction. "And it sounds like she has a really good dad."

"She's very special and she makes me want to be the best dad possible. Especially since I'm Mom, too."

He cleared his throat and excused himself to get more lumber. When he left the room, she couldn't help but compare his attitude toward children with Colin's. She shuddered and continued sanding.

Chapter 26

Joe had to admit to himself that he was disappointed that they were almost finished with the room he and Emily had worked side by side on all week. They worked well together and he had enjoyed chatting about everything from his plans for designing a little play house for Lily to her backstage stories about what the designers, hosts, and construction crews were really like on the shows she'd worked on. They swapped tips about the best ways to spruce up rooms, came up with some creative ideas for updating Evelyn's home over the winter, and even conspired to get some things done without Evelyn knowing.

Although there was still a slight stab of guilt, he found himself thinking about her and opening himself up to the possibility of letting her in, if she would have him. She appeared stronger than when she first arrived in town, but she had been through something horrible and was still probably carrying her own wounds.

Evelyn greeted him at the door with her usual warm smile and hug. He smelled apple pie baking and she gave him a wink.

"With all the work you've been doing this week, I just had to make you another pie. It will go nicely with the squash bisque I'm planning to make for lunch, if you'll stay."

"You know I never turn down one of your home-cooked meals. I'd better get upstairs and earn it though."

"The floor looks beautiful up there. It got me to thinking about the floor in the other room that's been closed off, and wondering if you had time to help Emily refinish it when you're done. I just had a call from another guest who would like to come for Thanksgiving weekend, and I can accommodate them if that room is available."

"Of course I have time. Anything for you."

As he leaned down to kiss her on the cheek, he saw a twinkle in her eye. *She's trying to set me up.*

He chuckled as he walked up the stairs. *The people of this town are conspiring to get me dating again. Okay, if that's what it takes to be able to do the things I've been wanting to do for Evelyn, I can play along.*

He refused to admit to himself that he was glad for an excuse to spend more time at the house – and with Emily – over the next few weeks.

Chapter 27

E mily was starting to get used to working with Joe most days. It was nice to work with someone who had such skill and technique and who wasn't mugging for a camera. He even asked for and listened to her opinions.

They were both glad that Evelyn was finally letting him do more for her and they had hopes that the house would be back to its former splendor and able to accommodate more guests in the spring. Emily had talked with Evelyn about how badly Joe wanted to do more at the house and reminded her that it would be a gift to him to let him help her in that way. She was again unsure if she had actually convinced Evelyn or if Evelyn had "given in" because she knew it would help someone else.

Emily found time with Joe refreshing. It was somehow healing to spend time with a man who didn't have an ego or agenda and who showed concern for the people around him. After the nightmare with Colin, she had started to wonder if any decent men existed apart from her father and brother. Watching him with Lily and his parents at church, she got the feeling that he was a lot like them. The only problem was that she didn't trust her feelings or her ability to judge men's characters these days.

She felt safe developing a friendship with him. At least, she convinced herself that's all they were developing.

∞∞∞

Emily had finally figured out a system for enjoying the beach in the cool mid-November weather. She filled her travel mug with hot coffee, grabbed her Bible and journal, and drove to the parking area that overlooked the bluffs of Lake Michigan.

"Lord, it's hard to believe I've been here for over two months. You did exactly what You told me You would do. You showed me the town I was supposed to move to and You made a way for me to find a wonderful place to live and new friends and a new church and a new life. You've healed me from my bad marriage and worse divorce and given me the chance to completely start over.

"I'm afraid, though, Lord. I'm afraid of my feelings when I'm around Joe. He seems like a good man who loves his daughter and his family and You. But I don't know if I trust myself to make decisions in matters of the heart again." *Trust who?*

She absorbed that thought for a minute.

"Okay. You got me out of LA. You brought me to a new town and gave me a new life. You healed my wounds and helped me grow. I can trust *You* with my heart. I wasn't following Your lead before, but I am now. I know You won't let me go astray and You won't let me down."

She took a deep breath. "As for me, I trust in You."

Chapter 28

J oe was excited to get up and showered on Thanksgiving morning. He had been sleeping better and he was feeling more ener-
getic and hopeful.

Thanksgiving was one of his favorite days of the year. As usual,
he and his parents and in-laws would watch the parade on TV
with Lily, and then they would head over to Evelyn's annual
Thanksgiving fellowship meal. Neither of his sisters would be
there this year, as one was at her in-laws' in Florida and one was at
her boyfriend's in Ohio, but many of the other regulars would be.

Evelyn had been hosting for as long as he could remember, and
he and his family had started going when he was a little boy.
When he and Janie got married, they split time between there and
her parents' house. He and his in-laws had gone together the first
Thanksgiving after Janie died when none of them could imagine
staring at each other and at her empty chair. Evelyn had made
those first holidays bearable.

He was feeling especially thankful this year. He finally admitted to himself and to God that for the first time in years, he was
developing feelings for a new woman. The guilt was subsiding,
helped by the conversations he'd had with his mother-in-law and
God over the past few weeks. He hadn't realized he'd needed his
in-laws' blessing to love again, but it set him free and made him
realize that he needed to get back into life. Lily deserved to have
the kind of life he'd had growing up, with both a mom and a dad.

He was looking forward to spending the day with Emily and seeing how she interacted with Lily and his in-laws in a casual family setting. It was important to him that they approve of her before he pursued anything. Today was a perfect, low-risk day for them to get to know each other.

"Daddy, is it time for the pawade yet?" He didn't realize she was awake already.

"Not yet, sweetheart, but that means we have time for a Thanksgiving bath before everyone gets here."

"I can use the pilgrim soap Gwandma gave me?"

"Of course, Princess. You want to be nice and clean before you put on your special dress."

Chapter 29

Emily loved Thanksgiving. She had returned to her tradition of listing as many things as possible that she was thankful for during her morning time with God. This year took longer than in the past because she thanked Him for everything from giving her a new town to call home to her toothbrush. She figured she had time to make up for and He wouldn't mind.

When she went downstairs, she was surprised to find Evelyn already making rolls and preparing the turkey. They had spent time the day before chopping and putting things into containers so that the day would go smoothly and food prep would take less time. They were determined to enjoy their guests and be out of the kitchen as much as possible. They had even set the table already.

The B and B guests were already out the door and with family, so Emily and Evelyn had the place to themselves. They poured coffee and sat down to watch the parade on TV. It was a nice treat to have no one to cater to for the moment, and she was looking forward to spending the day with their guests who would arrive in a few hours.

She was looking forward to meeting some people she'd heard about but hadn't yet met, as well as spending the day with Mitch, his sister and nephew, Ben and Rachel, a couple of the Bridge Ladies, a few other people from the church who had no family in town, and Joe and his family. She was especially interested in seeing Joe with his family. That would tell her everything she needed to know about him. She had stopped trying to convince herself that she didn't have feelings for him and started to open herself up to the possibility of trusting again. Even though she was going to err on the side of caution, she was open.

She was starting to think she knew what she needed to about him. The last bit of evidence that he was a great guy came a few nights before when she was bringing Evelyn home from Bridge Club and they passed the house he was flipping.

As they passed, they looked in the window and saw Joe and Lily ballroom dancing in the big front room. The electricity still wasn't completely finished, so there were candles flickering everywhere. Lily had a princess dress on and was wearing a crown, and it looked like Joe was dressed in a suit. Without thinking or saying anything to Evelyn, Emily had slowed the car to a stop and just watched, in awe of the sweet sight.

Evelyn turned to her and said, "We need to pray that God would make a way for him to raise that beautiful little girl in that beautiful big house." She agreed and they stayed right there in the middle of the street, praying fervently for father and daughter and house.

The image of them dancing stayed in her mind playing over and over like a movie ever since. *He's one of the good ones*.

Chapter 30

T he chorus of "Happy Thanksgiving" went through the room every time someone new opened the front door. This is what every holiday should be.

Emily was a little overwhelmed, but took in the room. Friends and family members who had known each other forever gathered as one with complete strangers and even newbies in town such as herself. Everyone treated everyone else as if they'd known and loved them forever.

She didn't remember the last time she'd hugged so many strangers; she was pretty sure this was the first time in her adult life. She wished her parents were there to experience it, but they were in Indiana with her brother and his family and they had promised that they would come to Hideaway for Christmas.

Even though she was feeling much more relaxed around Joe, she still felt a little shock go through her system every time he walked into a room. Maybe *thrill* would be the more accurate word.

When he finally came through the door with family and a truck load of food in tow, she felt like the room was complete. Little Lily was wearing her princess crown, of course, and had a very pretty burgundy velvet vintage dress on. Her Grandma Mary beamed as Lily told everyone that the dress was her mommy's and that her grandma had made it herself. How wonderful that they were sharing the mother she never knew with her starting at such a young age. *As it should be.*

Joe greeted her with a "Happy Thanksgiving" and a hug that made her knees go a little weak. She had prepared herself for polite hugs from strangers, but not for bear hugs from men who took her breath away even when they weren't squeezing it out of her. She had almost recovered when he gave her a little wink that sent her swooning all over again.

Needing to get her bearings, she thought up an excuse to go into the kitchen for a moment.

"Lord, please make him stop flirting with me! If I'm going to get through this day in one piece, he has to stop flirting."

"Am I interrupting anything?"

Oh my gosh, nan! Have some mercy! No flirting and no following me into empty rooms! "No, you're not interrupting anything. I was just coming in to check on the turkey and to see if anything else needed to go to the dining room."

"I thought I heard you talking."

"Oh. That. I was just chatting with God. You know, talking about my day, telling Him about the turkey." *Stop talking. You're embarrassing yourself.*

He chuckled. "I do the same thing. I think he likes it when we tell Him things He already knows." There was that wink again. Good thing she wasn't a drinker; she would be diving into a bottle of *something* right about now.

"Shall we?" He held open the door for her and she passed through with a dish she hoped was supposed to go to the dining room.

∞ ∞ ∞

The afternoon was full of food and games. Emily played Candy-land with Joe, Lily, and Lily's grandmother Mary, Euchre with Joe's father Doug, Ben, and Rachel, and Yahtzee with Evelyn, Mitch, Joe, and Joe's mother Sue. When the football game got into the fourth quarter and it looked like the Lions might have a chance to win, all the other games stopped and all eyes fell to the screen. When they won on a Hail Mary pass as the clock ran out, everyone cheered in unison and the room filled with high fives and hugs.

Lily fell asleep in her grandpa's arms and Evelyn offered her room for a nap since it was the only one on the first floor.

Chapter 31

As they sat down for the Thanksgiving meal Evelyn asked, "Joe, since you're the closest thing to the man of the house around here these days, would you say grace for us?"

"Of course. Heavenly Father, thank You for this wonderful day with family and friends, old and new. We take this opportunity to thank You for the gift of life, for Your gift of salvation, the gift of good food and conversation, and of course for the miracle of the Lions' win today. We especially thank You for Evelyn's generosity in gathering all of us in her wonderful home and making us feel like one big family. We ask that You would bless this food to our bodies and us to Your service. We lift this meal and this day to You in the Name of Your Son. Amen."

He was enjoying every minute of the day. From the way the adults all helped Lily play Candyland to the good-natured competition during Yahtzee, to having everyone cheer on the same football team, he felt like his social bucket was full for the first time since Janie died. He was glad he'd finally realized that not engaging in life or allowing himself to have fun was not making Janie any less dead and that he didn't have to feel guilty for being happy – or for developing feelings for someone else.

He was especially happy to see Emily and his family get to know each other. Lily really took to her and even let her wear her crown for a while. Since they had shared pie and apologies Emily seemed much more open, and they'd had many good talks while working on the room upstairs. They worked well together and had some laughs in the process, too.

The meal in front of them was a feast fit for a king. Everyone brought their favorite dishes prepared the way they liked them, which explained why there were so many kinds of potatoes and cranberry sauce.

Some of his favorite people in the world were around the table. Evelyn was in her element; she had the gift of hospitality in spades.

He remembered back to how much she did to help him in the days after Lily was born and Janie died. It was she who made schedules for people to bring meals and take turns helping with housework and grocery shopping. It was she who gave them visiting hours so that he and his family could rest, be with each other, and take care of Lily. He was a mess in those days, but she had made it possible for him to learn to be a father by taking care of the other chores that needed to be done so he didn't have to. And it was she who listened to him talk about Janie for hours on end as he processed through his grief and anger at God.

Eighteen months later he did his best to return the favor to Evelyn when George Glover died suddenly in his sleep. He owed so much to the man. George had taken Joe under his wing as a teenager and taught him how to do everything from small repairs to large construction projects. He stirred Joe's love for restoration and taught him pretty much everything he knew now that made it possible to make a living from flipping houses. They had bought the first house and renovated and flipped it together several years before and George encouraged him to turn his hobby into a career when he needed work that provided flexibility needed to care for a child as a single parent.

God surely blessed him the day they met. Come to think if it, he was probably about Lily's age.

Chapter 32

Emily was stuffed. This was the best Thanksgiving she had had in years. It reminded her of her childhood when all the relatives and anyone who didn't have someplace to go got together at her grandma's house. Evelyn was like her in so many ways. Even before Emily married Colin, the Thanksgiving groups had gotten very small as her brother and cousins moved around the country and started their own traditions. Still, those memories of the early days stayed with her.

As she leaned back in her chair, she thanked God for the hundredth time for bringing her to Hideaway. It was even worth everything she went through in LA. She would go through it all again to have this day with these people in this room.

She looked over at Joe and caught him watching her and smiling. Feeling peaceful and content, she smiled back. There was no fear, just peace.

She quietly got up and started taking dishes to the kitchen. Joe, Mitch, Rachel, and Ben quickly followed and insisted that the others stay put. Many hands made for quick work, and in no time at all, leftovers were packaged up and dishes were clean.

Emily was putting the last dishes into the cupboard when she realized that somehow everyone but Joe had left the kitchen.

Hello, stomach knot. I see you're back.

He looked nervous as he moved closer. "I've really enjoyed

spending Thanksgiving with you, Emily. And I've really enjoyed getting to know you over these last several weeks. I know you detested me at first, but I'm glad you gave me another chance."

She started to argue about the ridiculous notion that she had ever detested him, but he placed his finger gently on her lips. "Please let me keep talking so I don't lose my nerve."

She just nodded. His finger stayed put.

"I haven't asked a girl for a first date in a lot of years, so I'm a little rusty."

She nodded again, eyes wide.

"I know you've been burned badly and I don't want to rush you into anything. I can wait if you need more time. But can I take you out sometime? On a real date? With no Evelyn or room full of people or sanding tools?"

He moved his finger so she could speak.

"That didn't seem so rusty. I would be honored to be your first first date in a lot of years."

He took her in his arms and gave her a lingering hug like she'd never had before. She felt safe and secure in his arms and didn't want it to end. He leaned down and ever so gently kissed her on the cheek.

Chapter 33

Emily put the finishing touches on her hair and took one last look in the mirror. She had thought about putting some curls in it, but didn't want to look like she was trying too hard. She loved the way it looked when she took the time, but since she rarely did, it would definitely seem like her date today was a big deal. The last thing she wanted to do was put that kind of pressure on Joe or on the day. The natural waves she had were pretty manageable and she was able to give them an upgrade with a dab of molding mud that made her hair frame her face softly without looking like she was going to the prom. She pulled on her favorite black pants and the green sweater that made her eyes pop.

Looking in the mirror, she took a deep breath and met her own gaze. *You look good.*

She had learned a long time ago how to dress for her figure and had found ways to accentuate her curves while not calling attention to the areas that were a little more curvy than she wanted. She had made peace with her looks a few years back; she wasn't perfect or skinny like most people in LA, but she was healthy and strong. That was enough.

All he had told her about where they were going was that it was one of his favorite places to go in the fall and that it was on the other end of Summit County. He told her to dress warmly and to bring her camera. Since everywhere around Summit County looked like it was out of a postcard, she had a hard time imagining a place that would warrant special mention of a camera.

She grabbed the grey wool coat she had found at a resale shop and headed downstairs. She was trying her hardest to will away the knot in her stomach.

Evelyn was reading a book in the parlor when Emily entered. "You look beautiful, dear."

"I don't look like I'm trying too hard, do I?"

Evelyn chuckled. "No, you just look beautiful. Why don't you sit down for a minute? I just made some tea."

"That sounds great. I'm not sure why I feel so nervous. It's just an afternoon in some mystery place and dinner."

"Aren't you *supposed* to be nervous when you're getting ready for a date? If you weren't, the date might be a waste of time.

"I used to get so nervous before dates with George that I couldn't eat for the whole day. By the time we would sit down to dinner I would be so famished that it took all of my willpower not to eat all of the dinner rolls. It wasn't until we had been married for two months that I got back to three meals a day. I starved all through my honeymoon." She chuckled at the memory and Emily laughed with her. She looked Emily in the eye. "It's worth the nervousness to be with the right man."

"I'm afraid to even wonder if he's the right man. I know he's a good, decent, honorable man, but I'm afraid to hope that there is a 'right' man out there for me. I know I'm not the same person who picked so horribly all those years ago, but I'm still not sure I trust my instincts."

"Let me ask you something, dear. Did your instincts tell you that your ex-husband was the right man?"

Before Emily could answer, there was a knock at the door. "I'll get that while you get your coat."

Chapter 34

E velyn greeted him with her usual warm smile and hug. Her smile and the little squeeze she gave him on his arm told him she approved of him picking Emily up for a date.

"Where are you two off to today? It's a beautiful day for a drive."

"I wanted to show her the view from Bellows Vineyards while there are still a few leaves on the trees."

"Excellent choice, dear. You have a perfect day for it."

Emily appeared at Evelyn's side and his face suddenly felt warm. It felt surreal to be picking up a date, but somehow since it was Emily, it felt right.

He leaned over and gave her a gentle peck on the cheek. "Shall we?"

Chapter 35

When he placed his hand at the small of her back as he walked her to the truck, it sent tingles up her spine. He opened her door, waited for her to get settled, and closed it.

Keep it under control, Emily. Any schmuck can be chivalrous and romantic on one date. Keep your eyes open.

As they drove out of town, she realized the one thing she hadn't prepared for was being in such close proximity to him without the distraction of a home repair project. She could smell the hint of musky aftershave coming from his side of the cab and found herself inhaling deeply. *I'm about to lose it here, Lord. Please help me to carry on a normal conversation and show me any red flags I need to see.*

He pointed out some landmarks as they drove out of town, like the factory that had housed a few different produce businesses over the years, the baseball field where he and Mitch met as six-year-olds and became fast friends, and the old farmhouse where he honed many of his construction skills alongside George Glover.

"This town doesn't seem real. You're so lucky to live your whole life somewhere like this."

"It's had its advantages and disadvantages, but all in all it's been great. I'm glad I got the experience of living somewhere else when

I went to college, so I could make an informed decision about whether or not to come back. Even if I wanted to leave, which I don't, I wouldn't rob Lily of the chance to grow up here. She has both sets of grandparents, my sisters, and her aunt, uncle, and cousins on the other side of her family who adore her." He paused just as Emily noticed he carefully avoided mentioning his late wife. "That doesn't even begin to include the people in town who may as well be family, like Evelyn. Lily has history here. She doesn't know it, but I think someday she'll appreciate the fact that she gets to grow up where her great-grandparents lived and she experiences things in this town that her ancestors had a part of. Most kids her age don't have that."

Wow, cute and *sentimental.*

"That really is something special. Growing up in a suburb of Detroit, I only rarely saw someone I knew when I went to the corner grocery store. I can't imagine growing up in a place where I felt that sense of community. That's probably why I've always been charmed by small towns."

"You mean like LA?" They laughed together.

"*Exactly* like that. When I moved out there, I planned to stay for a year and then see where the wind took me. I wanted to experience the beauty, the weather – which by the way is really boring – and the big city lifestyle. I had a degree in accounting and got a job working for one of the networks that has changed names and styles so many times that I can't even remember what it is now. One of my roommates worked at the Home Improvement Network and she liked my design style in the apartment enough that she got me an interview as a production assistant on one of their shows. That got my foot in the door and I started working my way up to some different shows and titles. I enjoyed the work enough to extend my stay a bit, even though I still planned to leave. I met my husband on one of those shows, and well, the rest is history." She wanted to show him that she wasn't threatened by the fact that he'd had a life before they met, that he'd loved before.

"And now you're living in a small town in northern Michigan."

"And now I'm living in a small town in northern Michigan." She smiled.

"Do you see yourself staying here?" Was that hopefulness she saw in his eyes? Or was it she who was hoping that he wanted her to stay?

"There is a definite possibility." The wide smile that brought out of him made her heart leap a bit.

Chapter 36

The hills and valleys on their drive made it feel like they were in a different world. Most of the leaves had fallen, but there were still enough to fill the view with a smattering of color. The evergreens provided a beautiful contrast and prevented the landscape from looking empty.

This was the first fall since Janie died that he could really enjoy all of the beauty around him. He had come to think that the cloud that had descended over him after that day would be a permanent part of his life. When he realized that the cloud was part grief and part penance for being alive when Janie was not, and that the cloud was affecting Lily too, he made a commitment to find a way to get it out of his head.

He had finally accepted the offer he'd declined for far too long and he spoke several times with Pastor Ray. Pastor Ray had lost his first wife when they were young, too, and he was the one person who truly understood what Joe had been going through and the decisions he made. When he said that not only was it *possible* to find true love again, but that it was *good*, Joe listened. He knew the words to be true, because he had grown up with Pastor Ray and his second wife, Jenny, and their family.

∞∞∞

They came over the last hill before the vineyard and Emily gasped. "Wow, talk about God's handiwork."

"I knew you would like it. I love any excuse to make this drive in the fall. When the colors are at their peak, this drive is like an hour-long worship experience."

"This is what I missed the most when I was in California. I could go up to the mountains to get a snow fix when I wasn't working, but I missed fall."

As they approached the old winery, he knew he had picked the right place. The barn with the antique wine presses and assorted agriculture tools was like a portal through to a different time, and he wanted to show Emily some of the interesting renovations that had been done on the large home that had been turned into a restaurant and tasting room.

It was far more rustic than most of the wineries in the area, and that made this place his favorite. It was too cold to sit out on the large patio, but because of the way the place sat on top of the hill and the way the dining room wrapped around most of the home, every table had a great view. He was actually glad for the cold weather, because the fire in the large stone fireplace would complete the picture the old place painted.

Chapter 37

Emily was fascinated by all the tools and equipment that were displayed in the barn. There was a small section that had some furnishings and decor made out of repurposed materials for sale that made Emily wish she had a home to decorate. Someday.

"Someone has a real eye and is incredibly creative. This stuff is amazing."

"Wait until you see the dining room. It's full of this kind of stuff."

"I'm actually starting to get hungry, so I'm glad I'll be seeing that soon."

"Me too. Let's go."

∞∞∞

The meal was incredible. It was a small place compared to the wineries she had been to in Napa, but its rustic charm far surpassed any of those. The son of the owners had lived in Napa for a few years after culinary school and worked in a few of the restaurants there as part of his training.

He and Joe had been competitors in summer baseball leagues and high school sports, and had formed a friendship over the years. As he came out of the kitchen to greet guests, he looked their way.

His face lit up when he caught sight of Joe. "Hey, old man. I thought maybe you found a new favorite restaurant."

"Never." As the two old friends shook hands, Joe gestured to Emily. "Pete, I'd like you to meet Emily Spencer. Emily, this is Pete Bellows."

"It's nice to meet you, Emily. I hope you were pleased with your meal."

"Pleased would be an understatement. This was one of the best meals I've ever had. That salmon was cooked to perfection and I can't even imagine what was in the sauce. This is an amazing place you have here. I can see why Joe raves about it so much."

"He *should* rave about it, he *built* it! All the charm you see in here is because of him."

Pete turned to Joe. "Sorry to accept compliments and run, but I have to get back into the kitchen for a big party that just put their orders in. Joe, it's great to see you. I'll see you on the slopes when the snow finally hits, if not sooner. Emily, it was very nice meeting you. Please join us again."

As he walked away, Emily turned back to Joe. "You *built* this place? That seems like something worth mentioning."

"He exaggerates a bit and doesn't mention his part. I did the renovation several years ago, but he made all the creative decor in here and in the shop in the barn. We planned out the layout so that we could make his vision come alive for this place."

Annnnd humble. He just may be the real deal.

As they walked out onto the patio, Emily stopped for one last look out at the hills and valleys below, now cast golden by the setting sun. "So beautiful."

"Yes, so beautiful." When she looked up at him she saw that he was looking at her, not the hills. He put his arm around her waist and gently pulled her closer. He searched in her eyes as if looking for permission, then seeing it, he turned her chin up with his finger and lightly brushed her lips with his.

Chapter 38

*P*ace yourself, Callahan. You don't want to scare the lady off. It took everything in him to pull back from the brief kiss. He hoped he wasn't imagining her slightly leaning in before he pulled away.

"Thank you for coming here with me today. You're a really great first first date in a lot of years." He smiled and gazed into her eyes.

"You're a really great first first date in a lot of years, too, Mr. Callahan." She grinned right back at him.

He didn't want the evening to end. Now that he'd let himself feel again, he knew he was falling hard for her.

When he took her hand and led her down the curving rock-lined path toward the car, he walked as slowly as he could get away with. He wondered if she would notice if he drove ten miles an hour on the way home.

Conversation flowed easily on the drive home, and Joe tried carefully to steer it away from topics that would involve Janie. She was such a big part of his life, but he didn't want to shove her in the middle of this budding relationship. He'd heard stories of widows and widowers going on dates and spending the entire night talking about their late spouse. He wouldn't do that to Emily – she deserved to know that she was the only woman on his mind tonight.

A deer darted out in front of them and he slowed down to make sure there wasn't another following it. When it appeared clear, he continued.

"I'm going to need to brush up on my driving skills if I'm going to stay here. I'm used to dodging idiots in expensive sports cars, not wildlife, and the few times it's snowed so far, I've stayed off the roads. When I was living in Detroit everyone forgot how to drive in snow every year, so it was a madhouse on the freeway the first few snowfalls. I should probably get a car with all-wheel drive, too."

He gave her a lopsided grin. "Well, if there's anything I can do to get you to stay– I mean, help you get ready for winter driving – you just let me know."

Chapter 39

T he next few weeks seemed to fly by. It was hard to believe that it was almost Christmas already. Emily and Joe were going to Traverse City to do some Christmas shopping and to look at cars for her. She had been researching and knew what she was looking for, but there weren't a lot of used cars that fit her criteria available in her price range. They were going to talk to a friend of a friend to see if he had any connections so that she could have a safe car before winter hit much harder.

She saw him starting up the steps and met him at the door with a broad grin. "Ready to fight the Christmas crowds, Santa?"

"As long as you're there at my side."

She flexed her muscles. "I've got you covered. You have the list of things we need for Shelby's room, right?"

Shelby was Evelyn's niece who had just graduated from college in Tennessee, and she was coming for an extended stay at Evelyn's. She was driving and had been suffering from some health problems, so her timing would depend on the combination of her strength and the road conditions. She would be staying in one of the rooms they had been working on, and it was almost ready for her.

"Got it. The list gets shorter every time she ships more things to the house. I'm looking forward to seeing her, but I'm trying to prepare myself to not recognize her. My sister has said she's in pretty bad shape. It took her six and a half years to get a four-year degree because she could barely get to class."

"Well, at least she's coming to the right place. This town seems to have some magical healing powers, so hopefully she'll be on the mend soon. I'm glad that list is smaller because that gives us more time for the Lily list."

She was looking forward to helping him shop for the little girl. She had only seen her a couple of times since Thanksgiving, both at church. He was extra cautious about having Lily spend time with someone he was dating, and Emily loved that he was so careful to protect his daughter's heart. It was just another thing to check off the list: great dad.

They had spent many hours talking about his hopes and dreams for Lily and his fears as a father while working on Evelyn's house. She had shared her own devastation at finding out about Colin's secret vasectomy and the heartbreak of not having the children she'd wanted so badly. It was amazing what deep conversations they could have when they were sanding and painting and putting up fixtures. The activity seemed to create a safe bubble around them and they talked easily about hard things.

Except Janie. They never talked about Janie. She didn't get the feeling he was pining away for her, but it was definitely intentional on his part. That was the only yellow flag she saw with him. If they were to have a future together, Janie's daughter would be a huge part of it, which meant Janie would be a part of it.

The shopping trip was successful. Not only did they find out about a car that would be available in a week, they managed to find everything else they were looking for. Emily was thrilled to find a little yellow princess dress for Lily and looked forward to the tea party Joe had finally agreed she could host for the three of them.

They were both exhausted from hauling bags around and navigating through the crowds of people who were low on Christmas spirit.

"At the risk of sounding like a cranky Christmas shopper, I hate people."

He chuckled. "Me too. Let's stop at the coffee shop and get some hot chocolate for the ride home. Chocolate is a great antidote for hate."

"You're a good problem solver, Santa. Hot chocolate and a long drive home sound like a great combination to turn us back into nice people by the time we get back to Hideaway."

Chapter 40

The snow was falling in big flakes, which was perfect for Christmas shopping but not necessarily for driving. He never minded long drives with Emily, so it suited him just fine. As they came around the curve, they saw break lights, lots of them.

Emily pulled out her phone and looked in the GPS app. "Looks like the accident is around the next bend. Good thing we took a potty break and got hot chocolate before we left."

He sent a quick text to his mom, telling her they'd be later than expected. Emily looked pensive when he glanced at her. He was about to offer a penny for her thoughts when she turned to him and said, "Joe, since we've got some time, can we talk about Janie?"

When she asked the question, his mouth went dry. He wasn't sure how to have this conversation.

He cleared his throat. "Sure. What do you want to know?"

"Everything. Well, maybe not everything. I want to know more about her, though. I want to know what she was like. I want to know what your marriage was like. I want to know what *losing* her was like. I want to know if you feel like you've really grieved for her. I want to know how you plan to keep her memory alive for her daughter. I want to know if you can go on without her. Why don't you ever talk about her?"

Joe stared at the string of taillights ahead. He was relieved that she wanted to know about that part of his life, but unsure about how to share. "Wow. I don't know where to start. We were high school sweethearts, tried to break up when we went to separate colleges, which didn't take, got back together after a miserable freshman year, and got married the month after our college graduations."

Her eyes urged him to continue.

"We had a great marriage. Everything went along as we planned, right up to and including having a baby. Then suddenly everything went wrong. We were in the delivery room and everything was going fine. She was coming out of a contraction when she went limp. They wheeled her away and that was it. She was gone."

He wiped a tear from his eye and she handed him a tissue. He took her silence and intense gaze as the sign she wanted to hear all of it.

"We had no idea or reason to suspect that she had an aneurysm. Labor was just strenuous enough to cause it to burst. They had to do an emergency C-section and prepare her for emergency brain surgery at pretty much the same time. We had signed papers saying that if such an event happened, the baby's life took precedence. The odds were so slim that something like that would happen that it was an easy paper to sign at the time."

A deep breath helped him to continue. "We couldn't agree on baby names, so we decided that if it was a girl she got to choose the name and if it was a boy I did. We agreed that we would force ourselves to love the name regardless of what it was, and we agreed to keep the names a secret. I didn't know what name she had chosen, and she didn't tell anyone for fear they would slip and tell me and I would try to talk her out of it.

"I chose Lily because Janie's favorite flower was the stargazer lily. I bought those things for every occasion."

"That's perfect. It's a beautiful name and a wonderful tribute." She unhooked her seat belt and leaned as close as she could to hug him. "I'm so sorry you had to go through all that. I'm so, so sorry."

It felt good to cry in her arms. It felt good to tell her about the worst moment of his life.

He pulled out of the hug and blew his nose. "Thank you for nudging me on that. I needed to tell you the story, but I didn't want to push that topic on you."

"I'm sorry if it felt like I ambushed you."

"No, I needed a push. I was so focused on not making you feel uncomfortable by talking about her that I made you wonder if I hadn't grieved or if I was hung up on her. I'm sorry for that. This is uncharted territory for me."

"I know. Me too. What about Lily? Do you talk about her with Lily?"

"We do. Janie's parents do quite a bit more than I do. They show her home movies of Janie at her age and they have some of Janie's toys and dolls and even clothes that Lily uses at their house."

"I remember the dress she wore at Thanksgiving. She was very proud that it was her mommy's. It touched my heart so much to see that."

He nodded and she took a breath.

"So, what about the rest? Do you feel you've grieved for Janie? Can you form a life without her?"

The look on her face was like a punch to the gut. There was such caring, but such fear. He reached out and took her hand.

"Yes, I've grieved and I'm still meeting with Pastor Ray. I've come to terms with the fact that she's gone and that it's okay for me to move on with my life – I *need* to move on with my life, both for myself and for Lily."

He looked deeply into her eyes. "I'm happy again. I never thought I would say that. And to answer your last question, I *am* forming a life without her – with *you*."

Chapter 41

E mily looked at the clock. Joe and Lily would be there in a few minutes and she looked around the room to make sure she hadn't forgotten anything.

She had set the ornate round table in the bay window using Evelyn's finest lace table cloth and silver. She was glad that Joe had agreed to the tea party while they were still in Traverse a couple of days before so she could pick up a special tea set for the occasion. They found a child-sized set that was painted like fine china but made out of acrylic. He was sure that Lily would love the tiny pink and yellow flowers and it looked beautiful sitting on the antique lace table cloth.

Emily turned on some soft classical music to complete the mood just as they knocked on the door. Smoothing her dress for the tenth time, she took a deep breath. She was as nervous for this as she was for her first date with Joe.

Her breath caught when she opened the door to find Joe holding a large gift bag in one arm and Lily in the other. They were such a beautiful sight together.

"Welcome, Mr. Callahan, Miss Callahan." She curtseyed and stepped aside to allow them through. He looked her over and gave her an approving look that made her knees go weak and stomach do flips.

"Wow, you really clean up well, Miss Spencer. You look extra beautiful today." He leaned over and gave her a kiss on the cheek. "I love the curls in your hair."

"I'm trying to impress you." She wondered if her cheeks looked as flushed as they felt.

"Mission accomplished."

∞∞∞

"Miss Callahan, may I take your coat?" Lily had on the same burgundy velvet dress that she had worn at Thanksgiving.

"You look beautiful, Lily. Isn't that the dress that was your mommy's?"

"Grandma said I could wear it today because it's for special 'casions." She twirled to give the full effect.

Joe beamed at her. "We've seen pictures and she looks just like her mommy in that dress."

"Well, that must mean that your mommy was very beautiful, too."

Lily answered with another twirl as Joe and Emily shared a smile over her head.

Chapter 42

J oe took in the parlor around him. Emily had put an amazing amount of thought and effort into making everything just right. Along with tiny finger sandwiches, she had cut apple slices into hearts and stars and carrots into thin crinkle cut sticks. When he saw that she had made cinnamon apple tea from scratch and tiny lemon scones, he was fully impressed.

"This is all very fancy. If you ever get bored with accounting work, I'm sure Pete Bellows would love to have you work in his kitchen. I can't believe you even made scones."

"It's been a while since I've had a tea party, so I wanted to make it special."

"Speaking of that, I brought these to add to the decor." He carefully pulled the vase of red roses out of the bag. "For the hostess." He bowed with a flourish.

Next he pulled the package out that his mother-in-law had given him the day before. "Mary asked me to give this to Lily while we were here. She probably wanted to make sure she would have entertainment."

He helped Lily open the wrapping to reveal a book, "The Little Lady's Guide to Tea Parties."

Lily immediately took it over to the loveseat where Emily had sat down, handed the book to her, and climbed up on her lap. As Emily began reading, he was overcome by the sight of his daughter on the lap of the woman he was falling in love with.

He stepped out onto the porch, hoping the cold December air would help him get it together.

This just got real.

∞∞∞

After Joe gave Lily her bath and put her to bed, he was whipped. It had been a great day. He knew Emily was good with kids because he'd seen her with Lily and the others at church, but today when it was just the three of them, it was a whole different thing. It felt like they were a family.

He opened the large envelope Emily had stuck in his gift bag as they were leaving. He pulled it out and saw that she had created a business plan and two different versions of budgets. Then it hit him.

"She figured out a way for me to keep my house?"

Chapter 43

E mily fluffed the pillow on the bed and surveyed the room. It looked great. They'd finished it the day before and she'd had a fun time decorating it with Evelyn's beautiful handmade quilt, pillows, and accessories mixed with some slightly more modern amenities. The little arrangement she'd made with fresh pine needles and red ribbon made the room smell more like Christmas than paint.

She was nervous and excited to have her parents come to visit. She was ecstatic that they had agreed to stay through Christmas and that she could spend it in Hideaway. Her heart was full thinking about having most of her favorite people in the world under one roof. The only ones missing were her brother and his family, but they were with his in-laws.

The knot reappeared in her stomach when she thought about having her parents and Joe meet. She had promised herself that even though she was falling for Joe, she would listen to any reservations they had about him. After the breakthrough on their shopping trip the week before and their tea party the day before, she was feeling surer about where the relationship was heading and she was hoping they would see what she saw in him.

They would have a chance to spend some time with him and Lily and the rest of the family at Evelyn's tree trimming party in a few hours. Many of the others who were there at Thanksgiving would be there too, so it would be a low key and festive atmosphere. She was hoping they would arrive soon so they would have time for a visit before the other guests arrived.

Everything was set and ready for later. She and Evelyn had prepared all the food early and everything was neatly arranged in the refrigerator and on the counter so they could get it all out in a matter of minutes when the time came. Shelby was napping in preparation for the party and Evelyn was reading in the parlor.

As Emily was descending the stairs she looked up and saw her parents at the door.

"Merry Christmas!"

Chapter 44

The party was in full swing by the time Joe was able to get there. He hadn't anticipated having to spend more than a few minutes at the flip house, but then he hadn't anticipated a tree limb falling through a window, either. It was an easy fix, but he felt bad that it cut into his time at the party. He wanted to make a good impression with Emily's parents and he wasn't sure showing up an hour after everyone else would help that.

Get it together, man. Parents like you. You'll be ok.

He supposed that it was a little surreal to be spending the day with his own parents, the woman he was wooing and her parents, and his in-laws. Surreal or not, it felt right. This was his life.

Christmas music and the sound of laughter greeted him as he walked up the steps. He took a deep breath, inhaling the pine and cinnamon from the wreath on the door, and entered the house.

"Daddy!" Lily came bounding across the room with garland draped around her shoulders like a boa.

He scooped her up and swirled her around. "Hello, sweet princess. Don't you look festive?"

She pointed to her crown. "Miss Emily made me a Christmas Cown! Look, it has bewies and spahkles on it! Isn't it beautiful?"

He found Emily's eyes across the room and winked. "It sure is!

Almost as beautiful as you." He kissed her cheek again before she wiggled out of his arms to go back to where her cousins were playing.

He made his way over to Emily, delivering hugs and Christmas greetings along the way. He saved his best hug for her and gave her a kiss on the cheek and an extra squeeze.

"Joe, I would like you to meet my parents. Mom, Dad, this is Joe."

He shook Mr. Spencer's hand and accepted Mrs. Spencer's hug.

"It's great to meet you. Emily has told me all about you and you made her year by agreeing to come for Christmas." He gave them his most charming meet-the-parents smile.

"Well, we wouldn't miss the chance to spend Christmas with Emily in her new home for the world. She's told us so much about Hideaway and we're thrilled to see it for ourselves. What a gem of a town you have here."

See? Moms like you.

"It's been even better since her arrival." He flashed a smile at her.

"We were waiting for you to start the tree trimming. Evelyn insisted that the honorary man of the house had to place the angel on top of the tree."

"Well, let's get this tree trimmed, then!"

Chapter 45

Emily was glad to have a moment alone with Evelyn in the kitchen as the party was winding down. "Even if this wasn't the first tree trimming party I'd ever been to, it would have been the best. Thank you so much for including my family today, Evelyn."

"You are my family now, dear, and that means that your family is my family too. I'm so happy they made the trip." She handed Emily the basket of cookies she'd brought into the kitchen. "They seem to be taken with Joe, too. I noticed he and your father in conversation several times through the day. Your father looked the way my father looked when he used to talk to George before we were married. You're lucky to have a father who wants to look out for you."

Emily looked down. "I didn't really give him the chance to do that last time. He's probably been channeling his inner drill sergeant today." She was thankful that he was looking out for her and braced herself for what her parents would have to say later on. They were fair and were good judges of character, but they were also parents who saw their daughter get dragged through the wringer, so it wouldn't be shocking if they were a little hard on Joe.

Joe walked into the kitchen with an armload of serving dishes. "Ok, lady of the house. Your guests are looking for you to say goodnight before they leave." He kissed Evelyn on the cheek as she walked through the door.

"Alone at last." He drew Emily into his arms. "I've been waiting to do this all day."

"Me too. Has my dad been grilling you?"

"Not too badly. I'm taking notes for when I grill Lily's suitors. I just hope I'm passing his test. Are there any tips you can give me? I *really* want to pass his test." He wiggled his eyebrows at her and she giggled.

Emily heard a noise and looked away from Joe's eyes to see Janie's mother standing in the doorway. They separated like teenagers who had been caught doing a lot more than hugging and giggling.

Mary chuckled. "You two don't have to hide from me. I just came in to ask if we can take Lily home for the night."

"That would be wonderful and I'll pick her up in the morning. Thanks, Mom." He hugged her good night and she whispered something in his ear.

She turned and eyed both of them. "Please act like I never walked in and resume what you were doing." With a sly smile to Joe, she walked through the door.

Sensing Emily's nerves, Joe said, "I've told her all about us, and she's for it. She's the one who sat me down and told me to go find love again."

Emily startled. *Did he just say love? Ok, not technically to you. Settle down.*

She busied herself with napkins to avoid having to come up with words to say. *Lord, what do I say after that?*

He put his arms around her again and held her close. "Why is it that in this big beautiful house, the only place I get you alone is in the kitchen? This is the least romantic room in the house but it seems like it's the only place I get to do any romancing."

"Good thing you're so good at it. Imagine how romantic you

would be if we were in front of the fire."

"You'll see. I'm great in front of a fire. You don't even *want* to know about me in front of a Christmas tree. Now I'm going to go out and make sure my daughter is all settled and see how many other people I can either get out the door or up the stairs."

Chapter 46

It was finally just the two of them. Joe had busied himself with the cords for the tree lights while she said good night to her parents. Both were tired from their trip. They were easy people to be around and Joe had enjoyed getting to know them. They seemed comfortable with him and he hoped he was winning their approval.

"Did you catch any of that?"

"Any of what?"

"Come on, I'm going to be very disappointed if you weren't at least trying to eavesdrop. I've seen you tie cords up and it does not take you that long."

"Am I passing?"

"With flying colors."

"Well that's a relief. Now come here so I can show you how good I am in front of a fire and a Christmas tree."

She met him where he was standing – where he was shaking. *You can do this, man. Breathe. Just tell her how you feel.*

He pulled her closer than usual to steady himself and looked into her eyes. "Emily, my life started again the night you came to town. You didn't see me, but I saw you. I saw a beautiful, intriguing woman sitting on a bench eating a food truck taco and I felt things I hadn't felt in a long time.

"It shook me to the core that I would even notice a woman.

Then on the first day I was able to step foot in the church since Janie's memorial service, you were there right in front of me. Literally. And then you were the girl Evelyn had been talking about who had moved in. It was like I couldn't get away from you.

"I know God brought us together. He brought you here to save me from myself and to give me life again and to give my daughter a chance to have a family.

"Emily, I am madly in love with you. I'm not even going to pretend to deny it. I *am* going to kiss you now, though, if you'll let me."

"I'm madly in love with you, too. *Please* do kiss me before I die of anticipation."

And he did. At first he lightly brushed her lips. When she leaned in toward him he held her as if holding on for dear life and kissed her like he'd wanted to since the first day they'd spent together. In that moment he knew that he would do anything to make this woman his wife and to make her happy for every day he could have with her.

Dear Reader,

Hopefully if you've read this far, you enjoyed the book! I know you're busy and have other things (and books!) clamoring for your time and attention, and I hope this story brought a little brightness into your day.

Joe and Emily will continue to pop up in smaller roles in other books in the series and you can see their story progress along in the background while other residents of Summit County take center stage.

If you would like to leave a review on Amazon so that other readers can be introduced to this book, I would be so grateful. If having to leave a full review is just too much (I get it - they take precious time that could be spent reading!), but you'd like to leave a rating on Goodreads, you can do that too!

See you in Summit County,

Katherine

Summit County Series, Book 2

Trusting Again in Summit County

Rachel has everything she needs in life: good friends, a job she loves in the hometown she loves, a man who doesn't ask anything of her, and a box full of secrets in her closet.

Derek has nothing he wants in life: he hates his job at the family company, hates living in his small hometown, and has to watch the love of his life go on without him.

While Rachel works to maintain a controlled, if unsatisfying, existence that includes a hidden life, Derek makes plans to leave town and start a new life. God thwarts both of their plans and gives them a new opportunity to learn about forgiveness, trust, and taking chances.

Now available on Amazon in Paperback and on Kindle!

About the Author

Katherine Karrol is both a fan and an author of lighthearted, sweet, clean Christian romance stories. Because she does not possess the ability or desire to put a good book down and generally reads them in one sitting, she writes books that can be read in the same way.

Her books are meant to entertain and even possibly inspire the reader to take chances, trust God, and laugh at life as much as possible. The people she interacts with in her professional life have absolutely no idea that she writes these books, so by reading this, you agree to keep her secret.

If you would like to contact her to share your favorite character or share who you were picturing as you were reading, you can follow her on Goodreads, Facebook, Twitter, and Instagram, or email her at KatherineKarrol@gmail.com.

About the Summit County Series

The Summit County Series is a group of standalone books that can be read individually, but those who read all of them in order will get a little extra something out of them as they see the characters and stories they've read about previously continue and will get glimpses of characters that may be featured in future books. It is set in a small county in Northern Michigan, where everyone knows everyone else, so the same characters and places make cameos and sometimes show up in significant roles in multiple books.

This series is near and dear to the author's heart because she spends as much time as possible in places that look an awful lot like the places in Summit County. She is certain that the people who know her and/or live in the area that inspired Summit County will think characters and situations are based on them or their neighbors (or even on her) and she assures them that they are not. The characters and stories are merely figments of her overly active imagination. Well, except for Jesus. He's totally real.

The books are available on Amazon in both paperback and Kindle formats.

Books in the Summit County Series

Second Chance in Summit County

Trusting Again in Summit County

New Beginnings in Summit County

Taking Risk in Summit County

Repairing Hearts in Summit County

Returning Home in Summit County

Made in the USA
Lexington, KY
25 November 2019